# FIELDS' GUIDE TO ABDUCTION

A POPPY FIELDS ADVENTURE

JULIE MULHERN

J & M PRESS

*For my Family*

# ONE

If Chariss said it once, she said it a thousand times. "It's a good thing you don't want to be an actress. The only thing you're fit for is screwball comedies and they're dead."

Those words ran through my head.

Not the actress part. I didn't want to be an actress. That whole dive into real emotions and share them with the world thing? No, thank you.

But the screwball comedy part? Chariss had a point. My life was a screwball comedy.

How else to explain my current dilemma?

I was naked and locked in a bathroom. A man I'd sworn never to speak to again slept on the other side of the door.

I closed my eyes and saw myself as Kate Hudson which would make *him* Matthew McConaughey. He'd like the sexy part of that comparison. Even with my eyes closed I saw his slow grin—felt his slow grin. All the way to my toes.

Nope. Never again.

Never.

Today was the start of a new life.

No more drinking. No more clubs. No more sexy, dangerous men who were bad for me.

Especially not the one in the bedroom.

I crossed my heart, hoped to die (that might actually be happening—my head hurt that badly), and rested my forehead against the locked door.

What did I drink last night? I had vague recollections of a bar. Dark pulsing lights. Dark pulsing music. Test tubes filled with something sweet. The man.

The ridiculously sexy man.

Jake.

How many times could one woman make the same mistake? Apparently, a zillion.

Or at least three.

Why hadn't I grabbed my phone before my mad dash to the bathroom?

Screwball comedy. It was the only answer.

I lurched (Frankenstein, but less graceful) to the sink, turned on the tap, and drank deeply. Straight from the faucet. My mouth wasn't just dry. Dry would have felt like a spring shower compared to the arid wasteland behind my gums. I drank till my stomach sloshed then I ran my tongue over my teeth.

Moss.

Where the hell was the toothpaste? Not on the counter. Not in any obvious place. I rubbed a wet finger against my teeth. Better than nothing. Slightly. Then I held a hand in front of my mouth, exhaled, and sniffed.

Ugh. If I wanted to get rid of Jake forever, all I had to do was breathe on him. How was it even possible for breath to smell that bad?

I needed toothpaste and something—anything—for my headache.

Where?

The whole damned bathroom was white marble and mirrors (I would not look in those mirrors—would not). No drawers. No medicine cabinets. No razor or hairbrush or deodorant. No Ambien or Xanax or even Excedrin. Just white marble and a single bar of soap.

I splashed water around my eyes, reached for the soap, and sniffed. Jo Malone. Jake's favorite.

The man hadn't brought a toothbrush but he remembered his precious soap.

The scents of lime, basil and mandarin did nothing for the roiling in my stomach but I washed my hands and face. After I rinsed, the scents—*his scents*—lingered.

The towel I used was über-fluffy. Hotel fluffy.

A hotel?

Please, no. I squeezed my eyes closed and broke out in a tequila-scented sweat.

A walk of shame through a hotel lobby was more than I could bear. And if anyone took a picture… I rested my palms on the edge of the counter, opened my eyes, and faced the woman in the mirror.

A celery-hued paleness in my cheeks spoke of a wild night. That and the bags beneath my bloodshot eyes. I could pack for Europe in those bags. And my hair? I poked at it. Gingerly. As if my finger might get stuck. I'd crossed a screwball comedy line—Kate Hudson would never look this awful.

God help me if there were photographers in the lobby.

I wrapped myself in a towel, staggered to the door, and pressed my ear against its cool expanse.

Not a peep on the other side.

I cracked the door.

Thank God the room wasn't bright. As it was, I squinted into the lavender glow of early morning sneaking through the gaps in the drapes. The dim light revealed a dresser littered with glasses and a half-empty tequila bottle.

There. Panties on the floor. Bra, black against the bed's white sheets. Dress, draped across the chair. Shoes? I'd find them when I wasn't naked.

I tiptoed toward the panties. Tiptoed, because talking to

the man in the bed might be the only thing worse than my headache.

He didn't move. Not an inch.

I hooked the panties with my big toe (bending over wasn't an option—my brains might leak out of my ears), kicked them into the air, caught them and, using the bedpost for balance, slid them on.

With one hand still clutching the towel, I tiptoed to my side of the bed and reached for the bra tangled among the pillows. I tugged. And tugged. Dammit. I tugged harder and the wisp of silk and lace came free. I stumbled backward —*thunk*—right into the bedside table.

A glass teetering on the table's edge fell onto the hardwood floor and shattered.

The crash reverberated through the bedroom—through my skull. Loud. So loud. Loud enough to wake the dead. I didn't breathe. I didn't move.

Jake slept.

The tequila bottle on the dresser snickered and wagged a judgmental finger at me. *You're so clumsy when you're hung over.*

I narrowed my eyes and shot Señor Cuervo a death glare. Who was I kidding with the *Señor*? José and I were on a first-name basis. *Go to hell, José.*

What would I say if Jake did wake up? *About last night, remember when I said never again? I totally meant it. Now. This moment. This morning. Us. It's a mistake. It won't happen again. Ever.* He'd just smile that cat-and-canary smile of his and charm me back into bed.

Why? Why, why, why?

I knew better.

He knew better.

But my life was a screwball comedy so, of course, I'd gone to bed with the man who'd broken my heart. Twice.

I stood straighter. I was over him. Getting over him had

taken more tears, bottles of tequila, and quarts of ice cream than I cared to count. But he'd been out of my system. And now this.

If I snuck out without talking to him, my heart might not shatter.

All I needed was my dress.

A sea of broken glass separated me from the black silk. If I'd felt halfway decent, I could have leapt over the shards.

I didn't feel an eighth of the way decent. Every muscle in my body hurt. What exactly had we done to make my calves ache?

Never mind—*lalalalalala*—I didn't want to know.

If I stepped there and there and there, I could reach the dress without shredding my feet.

One step. Two steps. Thre—

"Son of a bi—" I clamped one hand over my mouth and hopped on my uninjured foot. Hop. Hop. Hop. Into the dresser.

*Thunk.*

Pain shot through my hip.

That would leave a mark.

The tequila bottle snickered again.

Well. José and I were done. Forever. I meant it this time (unlike those other times—those other times were passing fancies). I shot him another death glare. Done. Adios. Finito. Don't let the door hit you on the way out.

José smirked.

I planned my route to the damned dress. Just a few steps. Easy steps without a cut foot and an epic hangover. With both...

I had this.

Step.

Step.

One. More. Step.

I leaned. I reached. I snatched the dress off the chair.

Jake didn't move. Thank God for small favors.

I shimmied into my dress. Shoes? Where were they?

I looked down at my feet. A pool of blood had formed beneath my toes.

No way was I jamming a bloody foot into my new Louboutins. Maybe there was a bandage in that bathroom. At least there was a towel. I limped back to all that whiteness leaving a bloody trail behind me.

The bathroom really was enormous. The glass shower enclosure was larger than most cars and the damned mirrors went on for miles. And there were towels. Lots of them. They batted their eyelashes at me—a come-hither invitation. God, I wanted a shower.

As soon as I got home, I'd stand under a piping hot stream of water until last night's sins (even the forgotten ones) were washed away.

I crouched and poked on the flat surface of the cabinet below the sink until a door popped open. Inside, I found yet another stack of towels, washcloths, and an industrial size bottle of aspirin. Nothing else.

First things first.

Aspirin. I forged a long and valiant battle with the child-proof lid.

Victory!

I swallowed three pills, washing them down with more water from the tap. Then I grabbed a washcloth, sat on the toilet, and pressed the cloth against my foot.

It felt good to sit. Spend-the-day-there good.

If only he weren't in the bedroom, liable to wake up at any time.

I pulled the cloth away from my foot and eyed the cut. A shard of glass glinted in the morning light.

Hell.

I gritted my teeth and pulled the sliver out of my skin.

More blood. An ocean of blood. I should-have-grabbed-two-washcloths blood.

I pressed the crimson-soaked cloth against the cut. Pressure. That was the ticket.

And another washcloth. That was the other ticket.

I limped back to the sink, grabbed two additional cloths, and held them against my foot until the bleeding stopped.

Then I returned to the bedroom.

The light had shifted from lavender to lemon. And, God bless him, Jake still slept.

I spotted my handbag (a black clutch just big enough for my cell, I.D., and credit card) on the dresser next to the tequila. Where were the shoes? I wasn't leaving without them.

There. One near the foot of the bed, the other on the floor near his head.

I tiptoed to the shoe at the bottom of the bed, snagged the sandal, and hung it around my wrist from its strap. Then I crept toward the remaining shoe.

Got it!

Jake still hadn't moved. At all.

He was so deeply asleep I could brush one last kiss across his lips before I disappeared. He'd never know.

Stupid? Totally. What if he woke up?

But what if I walked away without kissing him one last time? A kiss I'd actually remember.

My eyes filled with tears. I blamed the tequila-induced headache.

I inched back the duvet.

Jake's head rested on a pillow and I took a few seconds to memorize his face in repose. He was handsome in a chiseled Hollywood movie-star way. His only visible flaw, a small crescent-shaped scar on his chin. The invisible flaws were many. I rubbed my eyes. I would not cry. Would not. My eyes were blood-shot enough already.

He was more trouble than he was worth.

He was too good looking.

He was not my type. (Liar, liar.)

He'd broken my heart. Twice.

I leaned down and brushed a last kiss against his cheek. There. Done. No reason to stay. But I paused.

His cheek was clammy.

"Are you sick?" My voice was hardly louder than the hum of the air conditioner.

He didn't move.

Of course he didn't. He'd slept through my shattering crystal and hopping around the bedroom like a demented kangaroo. A little thing like a whisper would hardly wake him.

The smart thing would be to sneak out. Disappear.

But what if he needed help?

I rested my hand against his forehead.

His skin was damp and waxy.

What was wrong with his mouth? Was that foam?

"Jake!"

He didn't move. Not an inch.

I poked him. "Jake!"

Nothing.

Oh my God. Oh. My. God.

I stumbled backward. My heart thudded against my chest. My lungs refused to take in air.

I collapsed into an armchair and pressed the heels of my palms against my eye sockets. One of my sandals scratched at my neck. I threw the stilettos onto the floor. Their red soles looked like blood.

With shaking fingers, I reached for the phone on the bedside table and dialed 9-1-1.

"What's your emergency?" The operator's voice was cool and professional.

"I need an ambulance."

"What's your emergency, ma'am?"

"It's my boyfr—it's my—he's cold and clammy and he's not moving."

"Is he breathing?" asked the voice.

"I can't tell—" my voice caught "—I think he might have overdosed."

"Do you know his name, ma'am?"

"Of course." Heat rose from my chest to my cheeks. I wasn't *that* girl—the girl who woke up with questionable men. Except, this morning, I was. "His name is Jake Smith."

A few seconds ticked by. Seconds I spent staring at Jake's pale face.

"Are you there, ma'am?"

"Yes." Talking required effort, and between the pain in my head and the pain in my heart, I was fresh out of effort.

"Where are you?"

I looked around the bedroom for clues. There were none. "I don't know." How pathetic was that?

"Are you safe?" the operator asked.

"Yes."

"What's your name?"

I could lie. I considered it. But my blood and fingerprints were everywhere. The police would find me. "Poppy Fields."

There it was—the pause of recognition. When your mother was one of the biggest stars in Hollywood, people knew your name. "I'm tracing the landline now, Ms. Fields. Help is on the way. Can you tell me what happened?" The operator was trained to keep me talking. I knew that. I'd seen it on one of those true crime shows.

"I woke up and he was like this." Beyond that, everything —the previous night, how we'd come to this place, what we'd done—was lost in a dense fog.

The tequila bottle shook its self-righteous head. *No one made you drink me.*

"Officers will arrive in approximately two minutes. Can you let them in?"

"Yes." I hauled myself out of the chair. My head objected. Strongly. How was it possible to hurt this much?

"Stay on the line with me, Ms. Fields."

"I'll be fine. Thank you for your help." I put the receiver back in its cradle and crossed the bedroom. The door opened onto a hallway filled with light. Wincing at the brightness, I made my way to the stairs. My hand closed around the bannister—clutched around the bannister. A wave of dizziness swept through me. I would not throw up. Would not.

The police were coming. I had to open the door.

Except the door at the bottom of the stairs already stood ajar, allowing a slice of sunlight to cut across the floor, sharp as the pieces of the broken crystal on the bedroom floor.

I collapsed onto the bottom step and looked around. I knew where I was—Jake's friend's house. I rested my throbbing head in my hands. Jake would be all right. He had to be. Our story couldn't end this way. Jake being dead wasn't part of a screwball comedy. Jake being dead was tragic.

"Ma'am?"

I lifted my head.

A police officer in a dark blue uniform stared at me. "Are you all right, ma'am?" His concern sounded genuine.

"Jake's upstairs." I gripped the bannister and pulled myself to standing. "This way."

A second police officer entered the foyer. This one regarded me with narrowed eyes, his gaze traveling from my bare feet to the barely-there length of my dress. The corner of his upper lip curled.

I read his nametag. Officer Crane.

How dare he pass judgment? It wasn't like I was a ditsy party girl who drank too much and spent the night with men I shouldn't. Well, not usually. And it wasn't like Jake was a one-night stand. He was an ex I'd hooked up with. Maybe. Why couldn't I remember?

"This way." I led the police officers up the stairs to the master bedroom. "In there."

They pushed past me, surveyed the bedroom (tangled sheets, broken crystal, and bloodied floor), and approached the bed. "Sir?"

"Is he all right?" He wasn't. But pretending felt better than the truth.

Officer Crane ignored me. "Sir?"

Jake didn't answer.

The police officer poked Jake in the shoulder and got no response (I could have told him poking wouldn't work). Then Officer Crane turned on the bedside lamp and took a good look at the man in the bed. The color leached out of Officer Crane's face.

What? What was wrong? I stepped inside the bedroom.

The police officers didn't seem to notice me. Their gazes were fixed on the man in the bed.

Officer Crane looked up, spearing me with a glare. "What kind of drugs did you take?"

I shook my head. "I didn't take any drugs."

"What kind did he take?" His lip curled until it kissed his nose.

"He didn't." That I knew of. "He didn't."

He snorted. "We'll see what an autopsy says about that."

# TWO

The sun setting over the Pacific gilded the sky and limned wisps of clouds in shades of crimson and bronze. The glorious colors reflected on the plane's wing. Breathtaking. It was the kind of sunset people from fly-over states paid good money to see.

I swallowed a yawn and shifted my gaze from the fading sun to the brightest star in Hollywood.

His disapproving gaze was settled firmly upon me. "Are you going to this resort opening because they're paying you?"

"Yes." The lie was a small one and easier than explaining my need to escape.

He pursed his lips. "If you're hard up for money all you need to do is ask." Then James Ballester offered me the smile that had melted a million women's hearts. "You know that, right? Anything I have is yours." James and my mother made four movies together. Each one grossed more than five-hundred-million dollars. *Anything* covered a lot of ground.

"You should be careful. Someday I may take you up on that."

He reached across the space that separated us and took my hand. His fingers were warm and dry and elegant. His gaze shifted from my face to the last rays of sunshine glinting off the plane's wing, then he reached deep within himself and found his soulful expression. If his smile didn't melt a woman's heart, the soulful expression would. Guaranteed. And once her heart was melted, she'd fall in line with his plans.

Even I blinked. And I knew the soulful expression was an act. A face practiced in front of a mirror until it was perfect.

His grip on my hand tightened. "I mean it, Poppy. What's going on with you? If you need money, tell me."

"I'm fine." And I was—at least when it came to money. I wasn't mega-movie-star-rich but I wasn't scrounging for my next meal—or even my next first-class plane ticket. "I hate flying commercial and when Chariss said you were going to Mexico—"

"Honey, you can use my plane anytime. I don't have to be on it." That soulful expression of his—it said he adored me, would do anything for me, would even give me an airplane and its crew.

There were three things the movie-ticket-buying public didn't know about James Ballester. One—he was genuinely nice. Two—he was incredibly generous. Three—he was gay.

America's heartthrob preferred men.

For all the talk about acceptance and rainbows and inclusion, women still wanted the man they were lusting after to lust after them. James was so deeply in the closet, he had one foot in Narnia.

He amped up the soulful look. His eyes shone. His lips parted. He looked as if he was about to offer to walk through hell and back for me. "Tell me why you're going to this resort."

"I'm doing a favor for a friend."

He raised a brow and tilted his head, a silent demand for a better answer.

I didn't have a better answer. "André promised them A-listers." Not a lie but not the truth. Telling the truth might break me.

Lying to James—I squeezed his hand—was *wrong*. When my dad disappeared, and I moved in with Chariss, it was James who acted like a parent. Not Chariss. Chariss never wanted to be a mother. Not when I was a baby. Certainly not when I was a teenager with an attitude. For nearly ten years, James, not the woman who'd given birth to me, had been the closest thing I had to family.

"André DuChamp?" James' lips thinned and the space between his eyes scrunched together—as if even the mention of André's name was distasteful.

James judged André based on his father's sins. And an epic flop was as big a sin as there was in Hollywood.

"Yes, André DuChamp."

James released my hand and crossed his arms over his chest. "Let me guess—the DuChamp kid didn't get any A-listers, so he needed you."

The DuChamp kid? Really? André was a huge success. He hadn't reached his quota of A-listers. He'd surpassed it. My friend was *the* agent to the temporarily famous. Housewives (both desperate and blogging), rejected bachelorettes, and Kardashian wanna-bes—they all wanted André representing them. And when they posted on Instagram about juice cleanses or charcoal tooth powder or their fabulous vacations, André made a cut.

Reality stars who auctioned off their fifteen minutes of fame on Instagram were one of James' pet peeves. André was another. "How much is this resort paying you? How often do you have to post?"

"It's not like that." The thought of escaping to Cabo had been so tempting—an escape from grief and guilt and loneli-ness—and all I had to do was pose for a few pictures at the opening night party. Thirty minutes of my time, and the resort would give me a luxury villa for the week. "Like I said, this is a favor."

"Forget about the resort. Come to La Paz with me. At the end of the week, I'll fly you to Paris."

Paris. Chariss was shooting a movie in Paris and I was supposed to visit the set. "What's this film about?" After a while, the films and the parts ran together.

"Chariss is playing a woman who pits herself against a drug cartel after the man she loves dies."

I laughed—a guffaw tied around a sob.

James' expression turned disapproving. "It's not a comedy."

I shook my head—the only apology I could manage without falling apart.

He tilted his head and the slight wrinkle between his brows deepened. "Do you think she's too old for the part?"

"Of course not." I spoke quickly. Decisively. Glad to talk about Chariss. Glad to discuss my mother's age rather than Jake.

Chariss and my dad met when she was eighteen and married in a summer-long fit of lust. I arrived nine months later. I wasn't a month old when a television pilot Chariss made before my parents met got picked up. Chariss was gone. It was Dad and me for fourteen years. When he disappeared, Chariss, who'd been passing for a woman in her twenties, had to explain how she had a teenage daughter. Making such an explanation hadn't made her happy. Nor did my current age of twenty-three. Neither math nor advancing years were Chariss's friends.

"Forty is the new twenty." I was willing to fudge math facts on her behalf. "She's still the most beautiful woman in the world." Why was I arguing her case? Any number of magazines had already decided that, despite middle age creeping up behind her, Chariss Carlton was more fabulous than ever. They trumpeted her ageless beauty on their covers.

Scribed articles about being sexy and forty. Chariss didn't need me—didn't want me—standing up for her.

"When you wrinkle your nose like that, you look just like her." James meant well. He did. But being a carbon copy of Chariss Carlton wasn't the bed of roses everyone imagined.

I wiped away the expression.

James settled back into the buttery soft leather of his seat. "There's something bothering you. I can tell. Level with me."

"I'm fine."

"You shouldn't go alone."

"I'm not. Mia is coming." Another lie. Mia, my best friend, was the daughter of a country-star who'd defined a decade.

James' gaze settled on the empty seat next to me.

"Mia takes two days to pack a gym bag. There's no way she could have made this flight. She'll get in tomorrow." What was one more lie in the greater scheme of things?

"I've got a bad feeling about this."

"I'll be fine. It's a five-star resort. What could happen?"

"You could be kidnapped."

"I won't leave the grounds. I promise."

"You could get food poisoning." Now he was clutching at straws.

"I sincerely doubt that."

"You could—" he shifted his gaze to the darkening sky "—you could need someone and you'll be alone."

Lately, that was nothing new. "I'll be fine."

James pursed his lips. "Mexico can be a dangerous place. So much violence. Did you see the news stories about the grain alcohol some of the resorts served? We won't even talk about the drugs."

*Drugs.* An open sesame word.

The police detective investigating Jake's death, Detective Parks, houdinied his way out of the locked steamer trunk in my brain and took the seat next to me. He crossed his left ankle over his right knee. He laced his fingers behind his neck. He leaned back in his seat. And he leveled his suspicious gaze right at me.

I ground my teeth.

"What's wrong?" asked James.

"Nothing." I focused on James and ignored not-really-there Detective Parks and his accusatory gaze.

"You don't look fine."

I forced a smile. "I'm on my way to a week of luxury relaxation." I couldn't afford to scowl at the phantom sitting next to me.

"Why didn't you bring that man you've been seeing?"

My heart lurched and my smile faded.

"Did you break up?" James softened. He was ready with sympathy or anger—depending on my answer.

The one thing—the one person—I didn't want to talk about. I shook my head, unable to speak. I'd be okay if I could keep the grief and guilt locked inside.

"Poppy." James' brow furrowed. His eyes questioned. "Tell me what happened."

I couldn't keep lying. Not to James. I swallowed the enormous lump in my throat. "He died." My voice was small.

"Died?" James leaned forward in his seat and reclaimed my hands. His face was a mask of concern. "What happened?"

My throat tightened and I tilted my head and stared at the ceiling of the plane. "He overdosed."

"Oh, honey." His grip on my hands tightened.

Guilt, tired of idly nibbling, sank its sharp teeth deep into my psyche and shook me like a ragdoll. It had been doing that a lot lately.

I'd slept while Jake's life dribbled away.

Infuriating Jake, with his golden hair and golden smile and devilish sense of humor, was gone. If I'd awakened an hour earlier, he might still be alive.

I freed one of my hands from James' grip and patted beneath my eyes.

"When did this happen?"

"A month ago."

"A month? And you're just now telling me?"

"I couldn't." My voice gave out and I gasped for air.

"You can't be alone." James never went anywhere alone. There was always a personal assistant or manager or agent around. Or me.

"I want to be alone." I snuck a peek at Detective Parks. For a figment of my imagination, he was awfully solid. His face was stony—judging me, my lifestyle, my values. At least he remained silent.

The words he'd said when he brought me in for questioning had scored deep wounds. Words like *accessory to a homicide* and *manslaughter*—as if I had actively taken part in Jake's death.

"Jake didn't take drugs," I'd insisted.

"Oh?" Detective Parks had packed more disdain in that single syllable than I would have dreamed possible.

"He didn't. Just party drugs." Jake didn't touch anything that could hurt him—not heroin, not meth, not opioids.

"So party drugs aren't real drugs?"

"No." So sure I was right.

"Party drugs are real drugs." Detective Parks had smacked his palm down on the table.

"Oh." A barely there *oh*.

He glared at me with eyes the color and temperature of ice chips. "There's a synthetic party drug trickling across the border that's five times more deadly than heroin."

"Oh." It was the only thing I could think to say.

"It's probably what killed your boyfriend."

Now I had no words. Not even *oh*. I'd simply stared at the top of the scarred table and let my tears fall.

"They're calling it Venti."

I glanced up at him. "Venti?"

His mouth twisted. "As if it's a harmless coffee."

"Oh."

"You could make a difference. Stop another death."

"How?"

"Where did he get the stuff?"

I didn't do drugs. Never. Not even Molly. Everyone had heard me say it so often, they'd given up offering me anything. I couldn't help the detective. I didn't know anything. I shook my head.

Detective Parks responded with an I-don't-believe-you scowl.

I'd gone home and cried—ugly cried—till my eyes were swollen and my skin was blotchy. I'd cried till the walls closed in then I'd walked on the beach.

I walked until my tears were spent, until my leg muscles shook with tiny tremors, until sadness nearly swallowed me whole.

Tears, walks on the beach, pints of mint chocolate chip ice cream, and fifths of tequila became my life. Day after day. Grief wouldn't let me go.

When André called and offered me this trip, I'd said yes. Immediately. Cabo. A place where Jake's memory might not haunt me.

"Poppy, you okay? You seem a million miles away." James stood, shifted, and sat next to me (on Detective Parks, who gave me one last this-is-all-your-fault glare before he dissipated).

I found a brave smile (James wasn't the only one who practiced expressions in front of the mirror) and offered it up. "I will be. A week away is just what I need."

His lips parted as if he meant to argue but he wrapped an arm around my shoulders. "Remember, I'm just a phone call away."

James' assistant appeared in the doorway and cleared her

throat. "The pilot asked me to tell you we'll be landing in about thirty minutes."

"Thank you." James tightened his hold on me. "I can spend the night if you want."

"Don't you start shooting in the morning?" The producer would have kittens if James showed up a day late.

James pressed my cheek against his chest and stroked my hair. "You're more important than a movie."

That had never been Chariss's philosophy. I leaned into his warmth. "It's a luxury resort. What could go wrong?"

# THREE

The resort's pool deck was spectacular. Tiered infinity pools spilled down the hillside toward the beach. The water in the pools matched the turquoise of the ocean.

I descended the stairs, pausing on each level until I reached the level with a bar. I approached the bartender. "A bottle of Perrier, please."

His eyes widened slightly. Even here at the tip of Baja, Chariss's face was still recognizable.

He handed me the bottle and I signed a room chit.

Then I made my way to the pool closest to the beach.

A row of chaise lounges topped with bleached linen cushions and carefully folded beach towels the color of a January sky faced the pool and the waves below.

I picked a chaise and unpacked my pool bag. Sunscreen, earbuds, and a novel. What more could I need?

It was only when I was hidden behind the cover of my book that I looked around.

Down the length of the pool deck, a large group celebrated the arrival of morning with tequila shots. Men with bellies or mustaches or large tattoos (or a combination of all three) were surrounded by beautiful women who hung on their every word. Their laughter and the clink of their glasses competed with the sounds of the waves.

I nodded once at a man (no belly, no mustache, no visible tattoo) who stared at me with a speculative tilt to his head. *Not happening, buddy.* I plugged the earbuds into my cell and drowned the group's noise out with Lorde.

The sun was warm—not too hot. The cushion was comfortable. I put down my book, closed my eyes, and let my mind wander.

It wandered right back to Jake. To the night we met.

He'd sent a drink.

I'd sent it back.

For most men, that rejection would have been enough. Not for Jake. I'd made myself a challenge.

He sauntered over to the table I shared with Mia, offered me a vague nod, then directed his sun-god smile at my friend. "I'm Jake."

The hit-on-her-friend ploy. Been there. Done that. Boring the first time.

I looked at Mia, "You ready?"

Mia dismissed Jake with a flick of her lashes. "Yeah."

We left him at the table and went outside where Donny, Mia's father's driver, waited at the curb in a Bentley.

Donny opened the door and we climbed inside.

"That guy was hot. You're sure you don't want to grab him for the night?"

"Please," I huffed. One-nighters weren't my thing.

"Do you want to go home?"

I shrugged and made a sound that could have been yes or no.

"I'd like to swing by Terra." One of the guys pursuing her was an investor in the club. Whenever she sensed he might be losing interest, she showed up.

"Fine." I made going to the hottest club in L.A. sound like

an imposition. "But if you decide to stay, can Donny run me home?"

Talk about impositions. The sudden stiffness in Donny's shoulders and the audible sigh from the front seat said the prospect of a drive to Malibu didn't fill him with joy.

Either Mia didn't notice or she didn't care. "Of course."

Terra was packed, but Thor (I kid you not) led us straight to a table in the VIP section.

We sat.

Mia looked around, tapped her fingers against the table, squirmed in her chair, and stood. "Back in five."

Yeah, right.

One glass of Champagne and I was out of there.

"If I didn't know better, I'd say you were avoiding me."

I looked up and there he was, offering me another sun-god smile.

"How did you get in here?" The VIP section at Terra wasn't easy to crash.

"I know people."

"A couple of guys named Benjamin?"

He had the good grace to flush.

"You know, this borders on stalker-ish."

"Me?" He sounded deeply offended. "Stalker-ish?" Then he broke into song. *Stay with Me.* And he sounded exactly like Sam Smith. Exactly.

When he sang the last note, there were fifteen women with their tongues hanging out of their mouths. I wasn't one of them.

"Pick from your new fan club."

His eyes sparkled and he gave the sun-god smile another try. He was—dazzling. "Not interested?"

"Neither am I."

He held his hands over his heart as I'd somehow wounded him. "I serenaded you."

"Nice trick. Does it work often?"

"Never fails." He did have a nice smile.

"I'm not a groupie."

"What if I told you I was the lead singer in a high school band?"

"High school bands don't impress me."

There was that smile again. He pulled out Mia's chair.

"And I'm still not interested."

"I'm—"

I waggled my fingers at him. "I'm. Not. Interested."

"One drink? Please?" There was something in the way he said please—as if having a drink with me mattered. "One drink then, if you're still not interested, I'll leave you alone."

He *had* sounded like Sam Smith. "One drink."

Three tequinis later, I had Donny drive me to the house in Malibu. Alone.

Jake and I met for coffee the next morning.

We met for dinner that night.

He took me sailing.

I took him shopping.

We went to movies. And plays. And concerts.

He spent the night at my place.

I spent the night at his.

He brought over a razor and toothbrush.

I took over a bottle of conditioner and a WaterPik.

He stood me up.

We argued.

He disappeared for a week.

I worried, then I listened to excuses, then I broke things off.

He begged for forgiveness.

I forgave him.

He disappeared again.

I worried, then I listened to excuses, then I broke things off.

He begged for forgiveness.

I didn't forgive him.

Our story wasn't even original. Not until the morning I woke up and he didn't.

"You are too lovely to look so sad." A shadow pulled me from my memories.

For one joyous second, I imagined it was Jake blocking my sun and my heart leapt. Then I remembered Jake was dead and my heart slammed back into my chest.

How could I have made such a mistake? The man in front of me was tall enough, but he was dark. Jake had been golden and sun-kissed. Their auras were different.

Despite the warmth of the sun I shivered

The tall stranger from down the length of the pool (the one with no belly, no mustache, and no tattoos) stared down at me. "I hope we're not disturbing you." He waved at the group at the opposite end of the pool deck.

Not till now. "Not at all."

"I am Javier."

"Nice to meet you." I lowered my sunglasses and looked up at him. "Poppy."

"Poppy?" His lips flirted with a smile.

My lips did zero flirting. "Mhmm."

"An unusual name."

"Is it?"

He nodded. A definitive nod—as if he was accustomed to having the final say. "You look like an American movie star." Javier wasn't exactly charting new territory. I'd heard a variation of that line one-hundred-forty-three times in the past month.

"Oh?" It was coming. I waited.

"Chariss Carlton." His lips stopped flirting with a smile and actually curved.

I returned my gaze to my book.

"You've heard of her?"

"My mother."

"No!"

"Yes." Here they came—the laundry list of movies including his favorites and the invasive questions. I checked my page number and prepared a yawn.

"Is she here with you?" Not one of the questions I'd been expecting.

I looked up from page fifty-six. "Chariss is shooting a movie in Paris."

"You are here alone?" He stepped closer—too close.

I pressed my back against the cushion and tightened my grip on the book.

An explosion of laughter had us both turning our gazes toward his friends.

One of the men (complete with belly, mustache, and tattoos—the trifecta—plus an ugly scar across his chest) had pulled off one of the women's bikini tops. He held it just out of her reach.

Granted, her reach wasn't far—not with her arms crossed over her chest.

Her gaze traveled from her missing top to Javier and me. She glared at us as if we were somehow to blame.

Whoever she was, she could give Chariss a run for the most-beautiful-woman-in-the-world title. Dark hair floated down her back, her face was a perfect oval, and her skin looked like bronze velvet.

With an explosive guffaw, the man with her top tossed the bits of fabric and string into the pool.

The woman turned her gaze to the water then stood. She stalked to the edge of the pool and dove in. A perfect, elegant dive.

A moment later she emerged from the water fully covered. Droplets from her body showered the pool deck as she made her way to the man with the belly and the mustache and the tattoos and the ugly scar.

She spoke. Softly. I didn't hear her actual words but the

laughter and the smiles on the faces of the people around her disappeared. Wiped away as if they had never been.

The man who'd swiped her top flushed a deep red.

She walked toward Javier and me with her head held high and her shoulders straight.

Her eyes narrowed as she neared us—eyes the exact shade of honey amber.

Javier held up a hand but she brushed past him as if he wasn't there.

He watched her walk away. "Marta."

Her step hitched—barely—but she didn't stop.

I had enough drama without borrowing theirs. I raised my book.

By the time he shifted his gaze back to me, my eyes were glued to page fifty-six. *Please, just walk away. Please.*

"Perhaps you'd like to join—"

My phone rang. *Gypsy* from Fleetwood Mac.

Thank God.

"I'm sorry. A friend is calling." Mia had a serious girl-crush on Stevie Nicks—thus the ringtone. I held the phone to my ear. "Hello."

"Where are you?" One day, Mia and her you-are-so-busted tone would strike fear in her children's hearts. Already I felt guilty, and I hadn't done anything.

"I'm in Cabo." And Javier was listening,

"So I hear. James called and wanted to know when my flight was leaving. He's worried about you being alone."

"I want to be alone." *Hint, hint, Javier.*

"Are you sure? I could fly down there."

"Positive. I just need time." I glanced at Javier. "Alone."

"I know. But why Mexico?"

"Why not?"

"Because, usually when you have a problem, you go to the ranch." Mia knew me too well. "Plus it's dangerous."

"Not at the resorts." I glanced up at Javier, who'd made no

move to leave. Obviously, the man couldn't take a hint. I conjured up an apologetic grimace and pointed at the cell in my hand. "I may be awhile."

"Perhaps you'd like to join us at the party tonight?"

Him and his oh-so charming friends? "Party?"

"The grand opening celebration."

That party. The one I'd agreed to attend in exchange for a villa. "I'll be there. Maybe we'll run into each other."

A flash of annoyance darkened his features but he nodded and sauntered back to his friends.

"Who were you talking to?" Mia demanded.

"No one."

"No one has a voice?"

"Some guy was hitting on me," I whispered. "He left."

"Then why are you whispering?"

"It's hard to explain."

"What are you doing down there, Poppy?"

"Like I said, I need time away." Then, because I didn't know how to quit when I was ahead, I added, "There are no memories here."

"They give you a villa?"

"Yes." A splash of uh-oh washed down my spine. "Why?"

"How many bedrooms?"

Uh-oh.

"I'm coming down there."

"You don't have to, Mia."

"I wanna come!"

"I want to be alone."

"Then you can be alone with me."

"Mia." Arguing with her was like arguing with a brick wall, but harder and less rewarding.

"I'll see you tomorrow."

"Mia—" exasperation curled my fingers.

"I'm coming. You can thank me later." With that, she hung up.

I stared at the cell in my hand.

Laughter had resumed down the length of the pool deck and I glanced toward the group. They'd returned to their tequila shots. Except for Javier and the man who'd stolen Marta's top—they were both staring at me.

Their gazes managed to be both hot and cold

I shivered and threw my things in my pool bag. I'd be safer away from bellies, mustaches, tattoos, scars, and tequila shots.

# FOUR

I sat at an umbrella-covered table on a sun-dappled patio with an ocean view and ate a light lunch—grilled shrimp and jicama salad—from a gold-rimmed plate. A starched linen napkin covered my lap. A crystal goblet filled with mineral water waited for my lips.

Turquoise waves lapped at a beach marked by the three bands of sand—dry, drying, and wet. Tiny white puffs, almost too perfect to be clouds, scudded across an impossibly blue sky. The sound of the water mixed with the swish of wind through palm fronds, the call of birds I couldn't hope to identify, and the subdued chatter of those at tables near mine.

There was not one thing to remind me of Jake. I thought of him anyway. Tears blurred my vision.

I shook my head, dried my eyes, and lifted a silver fork to my lips.

"You're Poppy Fields." An attractive woman with hair as white as the clouds planted herself in front of me.

"Yes."

"I once worked with your mother." She wore vibrant red lipstick which enhanced the smile she directed at me. "I'm

Irene Vargas." An expectant expression settled on her tanned face—almost as if she hoped I'd remember her.

I didn't. "I'm sorry but—"

She waved away my apology and smiled as if we were best-friends unexpectedly reunited after long absence. "You're too young to remember. I played the housekeeper in her very first series."

The series that tore our little family in half. The series that had mattered to Chariss more than her daughter. I'd not caught many episodes.

"How is your mother?"

"She's shooting a movie in Paris." Chariss working was Chariss happy. Chariss between roles fretted and meddled and worried about all the things I wasn't doing with my life. She began every sentence with, "When I was your age, I'd—" I could fill in the blank with won an Oscar, won an Emmy, or made enough money to last a lifetime.

Irene stared at me as if she expected me to say more.

I didn't. I couldn't. Chariss had never once mentioned Irene Vargas.

A few seconds passed by and Irene's smile faltered. "Well, please give her my regards."

"I will." I could be nicer. I *should* be nicer. "Are you still working?"

The smile returned to full voltage. "Me? I do a bit of television from time to time. But my granddaughter—she's the real star. Here in Mexico."

"You must be very proud."

Irene positively glowed with pride. "I am." The full-voltage smile found a few more watts.

"I'll be sure and tell Chariss I met you."

"You look just like her." Irene studied my face. "Such a beautiful girl she was, and so lost on the set that first year. I helped her. I told her the men to avoid and practiced her lines with her."

Chariss? Lost? Never. I swallowed a snort. "That was very kind of you."

Her gaze travelled to a table where a man sat waiting. He caught her eye, grinned, and tapped his watch. "My husband," she explained. "He says I talk too much." She shifted her gaze to the ocean. "You are here for a while?"

"A week."

"Then we'll see each other again."

I stood and extended my hand. "I hope so."

"We'll have dinner. I'll introduce you to my granddaughter. She's here too."

"That sounds good."

Irene returned to her husband and I devoured the rest of the shrimp, drank my mineral water, and reported for a session with the resort's personal trainer.

The trainer, whose smile was as sweet and melting as fried ice cream, possessed a sadistic streak as wide as Baja was long. I would do that one-thousand-two-hundred-thirty-eighth squat—or else.

When she was through with me, I showered and dragged myself down a sunlit hallway to the spa.

A masseuse led me to a dimly lit room. Somehow, I crawled up onto the table. With soft music playing in the background, she worked every kink out of my body.

Next a woman in a white lab coat came in, slathered me with algae, made me cross my arms over my chest, and wrapped me in seaweed until I was a smelly mummy. God help me if I needed to use the bathroom.

She fiddled with the dials on the wall and steam poured into the room.

"Fifteen minutes of steam," she said. "Then you relax for thirty minutes more. The seaweed will draw out all the toxins and your skin will be baby smooth."

Was there ever, in the history of the world, an aesthetician who didn't promise complete detoxification and rejuvenated skin? Maybe this one was telling the truth. Maybe being wrapped like a California roll would do that for me.

Probably not.

Forty-five minutes later, she returned and unwrapped me.

She put a large bottle of water down next to me. "Drink plenty of water." After promising detox and younger skin, "drink water," was every aesthetician's second favorite line.

I drank.

My lips left a black ring on the bottle. Blech.

I was undecided about my toxin level or the softness of my skin but the combination of personal trainer, massage, and seaweed wrap had replaced my spine with a noodle—a very limp noodle. Looking (and feeling and smelling) like a creature from a horror film, I oozed off the table and into the shower. I stood under the warm jets until the water ran clear.

I dried off and somehow jammed my jellied arms into a robe. Then I found a bit of strength and opened the door. One foot in front of another, that was all that was needed to get me back to my villa.

I clutched at the wall and shambled down the hallway, my gaze focused on my feet.

I walked right into someone. "*Oomph.*" I looked up. "I'm terribly sorry."

Honey hued eyes returned my gaze. Marta.

"I should have been watching where I was going. I apologize."

She didn't react. Maybe she didn't speak English.

I tried a second time. "*Lo siento.*"

Nothing. She pushed past me and swished down the hallway with even more force in her step than when she was storming away from the pool.

Well, then.

I shuffled back to my villa, stopping to rest often, wishing I still possessed a spine.

I fell into bed, slept for three hours, and woke to a mouth

so dry it made the Sahara look like a rainforest. I should have heeded the aesthetician's advice. I stumbled to the mini-fridge, pulled out a bottle of water, and glugged down the whole thing.

The bed with its crisp sheets and luxurious pillows beckoned—tempting me back to its comforts.

But—that damned party.

I sighed and headed for the bathroom.

My hair looked like someone had painted it with algae, steamed said algae, done a half-assed job shampooing (lifting my arms had hurt), skipped the conditioner entirely, then slept on it funny.

I took my third shower of the day, shampooed, conditioned, picked out the snarls, and dried my hair. Then I swept bronzer on my cheeks, mascara on my lashes, and gloss on my lips.

My feet (quite possibly the only part of my body that didn't ache) I slipped into a pair of gold Louboutin sandals. I pulled a silk slip dress the color of a tequila sunrise over my head.

Ready.

I strolled from my villa toward the main hotel and its pool decks frosted in fairy lights.

The scent of jasmine sweetened the air.

A crowd had already gathered and the clinking of glasses and the tinkling of women's laughter cascaded over the edges of the decks like bougainvillea.

A Flamenco guitarist played and, like the other sounds, his notes spilled toward the beach. Later in the evening, long after I'd returned to my villa, he'd probably be replaced by a club band—one that would have people dancing till morning.

I climbed the nearest set of stairs, ignoring the way my hamstrings shook with each step. One drink. A plate of food. A few pictures. And then I'd be done. I reached a pool deck, swiped a margarita off a waiter's tray, and sipped.

The crowd swirled around me. Smiling. Laughing. Eating. And most of all, drinking.

Another waiter passed by and I snagged a bite of ceviche topped with avocado on a tortilla chip. Heaven.

I followed the food.

"You are here." Javier's hand closed around my wrist.

Damn. If I hadn't been paying so much attention to the ceviche, I could have avoided him. "I am. Quite a party."

He shrugged slightly, clearly unimpressed. "You need another drink."

My margarita was half-empty. How had that happened?

He took the drink from my hand and signaled to a waiter. "Another drink for the lady."

The waiter returned faster than I could translate *por favor*.

Javier took the margarita from the waiter's tray and handed it to me.

"Thank you."

Javier claimed a glass for himself. "To the most beautiful woman here tonight."

Men who said things like that made my skin crawl.

He smiled at me. "Tell me more about yourself."

I took a tiny sip of my new drink and shook my head. "I should probably find the resort's publicity people. I promised to do a few pictures for them."

Javier's smile disappeared, replaced by an expression I couldn't read. Furrowed brow. Pursed lips. Was he pouting? Was he angry?

Maybe having Mia come down here wasn't such a bad idea. At least I'd have someone to run interference for me.

"I should go." I retreated a step.

"I will find you later." The coldness in his voice made it sound like a threat.

I merely smiled and slipped farther away from him.

I let the crowd carry me along like a skiff on the ocean. The tide of people deposited me near a railing overlooking the Pacific. The sun was setting in a blaze of reds and pinks and bronze. A golden pathway burned across the rose-tinged water.

"Beautiful," someone nearby whispered.

I looked away and took a deep drink of margarita.

The sunset, the party, the smell of the ocean, the way the warm breeze ruffled against my skin—it was all too damned romantic. My heart hurt from all that romance—hurt far worse than my aching muscles. Missing Jake was as tangible as the railing beneath my fingers or the glass in my hands, as painful as anything I'd ever experienced.

I would not cry. Would. Not. Deep breaths. Slow deep breaths.

"Miss Fields, may we grab you for a few pictures?"

A young woman clutching a clipboard stood in front of me. I'd never before felt gratitude to a publicity girl but I did then. I needed a distraction. Desperately. And when the pictures were done, I could leave. I smiled at her. "Of course. Anything you want."

She blinked as if my being easy to deal with was a surprise.

"Just tell me where to go."

"Right this way." She pointed to a grouping that included a rising Hollywood actor, a reality star who was rumored to make millions off her Instagram posts, and the woman from the pool and spa, Marta.

I followed the girl with the clipboard to the little group. She took my empty glass and told all of us where to stand. We huddled together as if we'd been friends since birth. We admired the last rays of the sunset. A fresh tray of drinks arrived and we toasted the fabulousness of the resort.

Marta actually smiled at me.

I smiled back and we clinked the rims of our glasses.

Shutters clicked—snap, snap, snap.

The cameras might capture our smiles but I caught a flash

of exhaustion in Marta's eyes. She frowned as if she realized she'd showed me too much and turned to the Instagram Princess.

I stared out at the ocean. Coming to this place had been a mistake. I couldn't outrun sadness. If anything, I felt more alone than I had at home.

I wanted to get away from the laughter and the smiles and the music. I wanted a locked door and a box of Kleenex. I wanted Jake.

The Instagram Princess pulled me into another picture and air-kissed my cheek. What show had she been on? Nothing memorable. Well, nothing I could remember.

"You'll come out on the yacht with us tomorrow?" she asked. My new best friend.

"I may have a friend flying in. I'll let you know."

That's when I saw him.

Him!

He'd fixed his gaze on someone and he was staring as if his life depended on it.

Jake.

It couldn't be him.

Jake was dead.

I rubbed my eyes. I blinked. It had to be a trick of the light. That or someone who looked

*exactly* like him.

Or maybe my heart was playing tricks on me.

Except—the way he tilted his head, the way he rubbed the tip of his nose with the back of his hand.

It was Jake.

I pushed toward him, weaving through the crowd.

A woman in last season's Prada stepped in front of me and I bumped into her.

Her drink sloshed over its rim. "Watch where you're going. Do you have any idea how much I paid for this dress?"

Please. Last season. I gritted my teeth and shifted my gaze to her annoyed face. "I'm so sorry."

"You should be," she snapped.

I could argue with her or I could find Jake. Jake won. Hands down.

"Really, I apologize." I looked back to where he'd been standing.

But Jake was gone.

Almost as if I'd imagined him.

# FIVE

"Where is he?"

A waitress stared at me with wide eyes as if I were a crazy American—one who'd taken too many drugs or drunk too much tequila or just lost her mind. Possibly all three.

"Where is he?" My voice rose. My gaze darted here, there, everywhere.

"*Quién?*"

"The man who was standing right there." I pointed to the exact spot. "American. Tall." I lifted my hand and showed her how tall. "Blond." I touched my hair, which was brown—so that probably wasn't helpful.

She shook her head. Had she not seen him? Or, did she not understand me?

I took a breath. "*El americano que estaba aquí.*" My Spanish was embarrassingly bad. "*Dónde está?*"

"*No sé.*" She backed away from me.

I turned a full circle, scanning the crowd. Jake wasn't there.

My lungs deflated

I'd made a mistake. A crazy, stupid, heart-breaking

mistake. Jake was dead. I knew that. I knew it, but I couldn't stop looking for him. I completed another circle.

A hand closed on my arm. "Poppy."

I wheeled around with my heart in my throat.

Tall. Blond. Not Jake.

Mike Wilde had his fingers wrapped around my arm. His brows were drawn together as if I'd worried him. "You okay?"

Mike's father was an actor (two movies with Chariss). Mike was an actor (zero movies with Chariss). Mike's father got paid eight-figures per movie. Thus far, Mike hadn't broken through.

"I saw Jake." The words slipped past my lips and hung forlornly in the air. It was official—I'd lost my mind.

"Your boyfriend? Is he here?"

No. Jake was supposed to be dead. But Mike was Mia's friend more than he was mine. There was no reason he'd know Jake had died.

"Seriously, where is he?" Now Mike's gaze scanned the crowd. "I'd like to meet this guy."

My eyes welled.

"Poppy, what's wrong?" Mike tilted his head and narrowed his eyes. "He didn't hurt you, did he?"

"No."

"Because, if he did." Mike suddenly looked very fierce.

"He didn't. I promise. I'm fine."

Mike stared at me, assessing. "Let's get you a drink."

"I'm fine," I repeated.

"You don't look fine." His voice was soft. Gentle. "Not at all."

I shook my head. Bit my lip. Scanned the crowd.

"What's wrong?"

"I'm just feeling a little down." Not exactly a lie. Every muscle in my body hurt, plus my feet were complaining (the Louboutins had been a mistake), plus I was seeing dead people, plus that whole bottomless well of sadness thing. All that together definitely weighed a woman down.

"I've got just the thing to make you feel better." He dug in his pocket.

"That's okay, I don't need anything."

He dug.

"Really, it's okay." Unless he pulled out a Lifesaver or a Tootsie Roll, I wasn't interested.

"No, no. You gotta try this." He thrust his hand toward me and a little coffee-colored pill bounced on his palm.

"No thanks. I'm good."

"You're sure?"

I nodded. "What is it?"

He shrugged and returned the pill to his pocket. "The latest party drug. Let's see about finding you a drink."

"Wait. Is that a Venti?"

"Yeah."

"Mike, I've heard awful things about that stuff. You're not taking it, are you?"

"It's not a big deal, Poppy."

It was. "Seriously, Mike. People are dying."

"Lighten up." He led me to the nearest bar. "What'll it be?"

"Just water."

"That's it?" His brows rose. "Open bar."

"That's it."

"If you say so." He ordered a bottle of water for me and a shot of Don Julio tequila for himself. "What are you doing here?"

"I flew down for the opening." I accepted the water bottle he held out to me. "What about you?"

"There's a tequila company looking for investors. They brought a group of us down on a junket." He held up the shot glass and eyed the liquid inside with narrowed eyes.

Owning a winery or a tequila distillery—the latest Hollywood status symbol.

"So, where's Jake? I wanna meet him."

My gaze traveled back to the spot where Jake had stood. The walls around my sanity were crumbling like sandcastles in the rain. "He was right there."

"We'll find him." Mike sipped his drink and smiled.

No. We wouldn't find him. Jake was dead and I needed my head examined.

I opened my water bottle and drank.

"Can we grab another picture?" Clipboard-girl stood right in front of me. Again.

Mike wrapped his arm around my shoulders and grinned at the camera.

I managed a smile—I was Chariss's daughter—I could *act* happy.

The woman with the clipboard thanked us and hurried off in search of the next celebrity on her list.

"You know, Mike. I think I might turn in."

"The sun's barely down." A naughty smile lit his face. "Oh. I get it. You and Jake have a good night."

I didn't have the energy to explain. Not about seeing dead people.

"Can I walk you to your room?"

"I'm in one of the villas."

"The ones with the private pools?

"Yes."

"Fancy. I just have a suite."

"Poor you. Good luck with your tequila people."

"Yeah." He looked over my shoulder, already in search of who he'd talk to next. "See you later."

I reached up on my tiptoes, kissed his cheek, and left him at the bar.

The crowd had thickened and all around me smiling people drank exotic cocktails and preened.

I slipped past them. Alone in a crowd.

"Poppy!"

Seriously? Could I not walk five steps without being recognized and stopped?

I turned.

Mike had followed me. "I just got a text from Mia. She's coming tomorrow."

"She's staying in my villa." I looked up at his smiling face —at a smile that looked more genuine than any he'd shared with me thus far. "I'm sorry. I should have told you."

"No worries." His grin widened. "I'm taking you guys to dinner tomorrow night. Bring Jake."

"Text me later and we'll set it up." I side-stepped away. Slowly. My feet now hurt worse than my hamstrings—maybe four-inch heels had been a bad idea. "Goodnight."

I resumed my push through the crowd.

"Poppy?"

Again?

I turned and stared up at a man who looked vaguely familiar. Dark hair, strong jaw, and very white teeth. I knew him. Somehow. "Hi," I said brightly. "It's nice to see you." What was his name? I searched my memory. Nothing.

He extended a hand. "Brett Cannon. We met on your mother's set last summer. For the movie she shot in Melbourne."

A surge of gratitude warmed me. If I had a dollar for every conversation I'd had with people whose names were complete mysteries, I could buy my own private jet.

Brett Cannon. Private banker from a bank in Hong Kong of all places. He'd been star-struck, ping-ponging around the set, and getting on everyone's last nerve. Since he'd been there at the behest of one of the film's investors, everyone had gritted their teeth and endured his inane conversation.

Brett claimed my hand and pumped my arm. "I didn't think I'd know anyone here."

How lucky we were to have run into each other. Brett Cannon was the mushy, too sweet cherry on the melting ice cream sundae of my week. I could at least be polite. "What brings you here?"

"One of my clients is an investor. Great place, huh?"

"Great." I glanced around us. Beautifully dressed beautiful people were sipping drinks like they'd never get another chance. "Really great."

He blinked at my lack of enthusiasm.

"It is great. It really is." Why did I feel the need to placate him? "I'm not feeling well, so it's hard to muster the excitement this place deserves."

His face cleared.

"Listen, Brett. I really don't feel well and—"

"Did you drink the water?"

I held up my bottle. "No. I just don't feel well and—"

"Because everyone says not to drink the water." He nodded sagely.

"It's not the water. I didn't drink the water."

"Then what's wrong? The food here is excellent. It couldn't be the food."

"I'm sure it's not the food. I—"

"Everything I've eaten has been top-notch."

"Yes."

"Then what's wrong? If there's anything wrong, you've gotta tell me. It's important that this week—" he waved his arm, a grand gesture that encompassed everything from the hotel to the cabanas on the beach "—be a huge success."

It wasn't the water or the food or the service—I was seeing dead people. "Too much sun and too much time spent with the resort's personal trainer."

"Rosa?"

Rosa, the sadist with a sweet smile. "That's her name. She's tough." A massive understatement.

"I was supposed to work out with her in the morning but —" he held up his drink "—I think I'll cancel."

"Wise move." I edged a step away. "If you'll excuse me, I'm going to turn in."

For a half-second Brett's face darkened—or maybe it was a trick of the shifting fairy lights. "It's early. You won't have one drink with me?"

Again, I held up my half-full water bottle. "Not tonight."

"Just one drink? Please?" He flashed his white teeth at me. "I was in Dubai last week. I'd love to tell you about it."

God forbid. My eyes glazed at the mere thought.

"Really, it's the best story. I was meeting with a Saudi prince and—"

"Brett, not tonight." I shook my head and winced like there was an ice pick in my skull, then, in case he missed the hint (entirely possible) I crossed my arms over my lower abdomen and groaned. "Maybe you can tell me tomorrow. Right now, I need to lie down."

"Let me walk you to your room."

"No. Thanks, but no."

I hunched over and took a few slow steps, then, over my shoulder, I said, "Goodnight."

I felt his gaze on me as I walked away. I stumbled through the crowd—method acting a woman with a stomach ache.

I didn't stop walking—not till the party was well behind me. Only then did my back straighten.

The sounds of the night—the occasional bird call, the hum of insects, the breeze rustling the palm fronds—were louder now. Or perhaps they were the same and the sounds from the party were farther away.

The warm breeze caressed my skin.

A shiver raced down my spine.

I paused and glanced over my shoulder. No one was there. No one. But my skin prickled with the weight of someone's gaze.

First I'd seen Jake and now this feeling of being watched—being hunted. I was being ridiculous. I took a tiny step.

*Crack!*

A sound that didn't belong.

My heart lurched toward my throat.

I stopped again.

Looked around again.

Saw no one again.

"You're being stupid," I muttered under my breath.

I felt stupid. And achy. And paranoid. And—there was that visceral shiver again—afraid.

I hurried down the path toward my villa.

Alone.

I should have let Mike escort me to my door.

Even Brett would have been better than the dread that walked beside me.

*Crack!*

"Hello?" I hated that my voice shook. I breathed deep. "Is someone out there?"

The night answered with its usual sounds.

My dad had been an Army Ranger and he'd started me in Krav Maga classes as soon as I was old enough to kick. As a fearless thirteen-year-old, I'd known exactly how to protect myself. But I'd moved in with Chariss and the woman I'd become was achy, out of practice, and scared.

My father's ghost appeared before me on the path and shook his head in disappointment. How had I let this happen? His daughter should know how to take care of herself, protect herself.

Great, now I was seeing two dead people.

I pushed past the man who wasn't there, ran the remaining distance to my villa, locked myself inside, and leaned on the door until my heart stopped hammering in my chest. It took a long, long time.

# SIX

When my heart stopped thumping, I kicked off my shoes, flexed my toes, and checked every lock on every door and window in the villa.

I toyed with the idea of requesting hotel security come and park themselves in a golf cart in front of my door for the night.

I rejected the idea—mainly because it was *exactly* the kind of diva-on-steroids thing Chariss would do.

Instead, I collapsed on the couch and studied my surroundings. The ocean-side wall was glass with doors that folded back to allow the breeze inside. Those doors (locked now—I checked three times) opened onto a pool deck where chaises waited for guests eager to soak up the sun or lounge at a shaded table beneath the pergola. Of course there was a spectacular view. Even now—at night—the moonlight on the water was breathtaking and the lights from other resorts looked like jewels set in black velvet.

Next to the living area was my bedroom. It too opened onto the deck.

Upstairs were two bedrooms with balconies. Everything was tasteful—from the terra cotta Saltillo tiles on the floor to the Spanish Colonial antiques interspersed with comfortable furniture.

This was a place designed for relaxation not rampant heart rates and shudders.

I breathed. Slowly. Deeply.

I listened. Hard.

I heard nothing—not so much as a peep—so I changed my clothes and crawled in bed.

I left the bedside table light on until it occurred to me that someone on the deck would be able to see right into the bedroom. I flipped the light off, hauled myself out of bed, and stood at the door searching the darkness.

Nothing. Well, nothing but moonlit water and expensive landscaping.

My imagination was obviously working overtime. First Jake, now a phantom stalker.

Back in bed, I considered turning on the lights, and didn't. Instead, I listened to the gentle whish of the overhead fan and let my eyes close.

*Bam! Bam!*

I levitated off the mattress, squinted at the clock—I'd slept for three hours—and searched in the darkness for something to throw over my nightgown. I also stubbed my toe on the bedpost, hopped around on one foot, and swore like a sailor.

*Bam! Bam!*

"Coming!" My voice was loud enough for the people at the hotel up the hill to hear the irritation in my tone.

Still half-asleep, I stumbled into the living area and closed my hand around the door handle. "Who is it?"

"Marta Vargas."

"Who?" And why in the world was she at my door?

"Marta Vargas." The voice outside combined desperation and fear. "Please, let me in."

Leaving the chain in place, I cracked the door.

The woman from the pool and spa stood on the other

side. Her hair was a tangled mess, her black silk dress (Gucci —this year's) hung askew, and bruises circled her upper arm.

"Please, I need your help."

"Just a minute." I closed the door, released the chain, and opened the door.

Marta pushed past me, slammed the door shut, and locked it. Then she surveyed my villa.

What the hell was going on? "What do you—"

"Are there curtains?" she demanded.

I stared at her. "What?"

She rushed across the room and pulled the linen drapes over the glass doors to the pool deck.

I scrubbed my eyes with my fists. "What are you doing here?"

She turned and looked at me with wild eyes. "My grand-mother said I could trust you."

"Who's your grandmother?"

"Irene Vargas." Irritation was edging out fear in her voice.

I should have put two and two together. "What are you doing here?"

"I need your help."

She'd already said that. I needed to sit. I plopped onto the couch. "Slowly. Please. Explain."

"He is a dangerous man."

My sleep-fuddled brain latched onto an idea—Javier. My gaze latched onto her arm. "He hits you?"

"No." She shook her head—an annoyed shake. "But he may kill me. I heard you arrived here in a private plane. Is it still here? Can you get me out of Mexico?"

I sat on the couch—lumps on logs had better cognitive abilities—and gaped at her.

"Wake up!" She snapped her fingers in front of my face. "We don't have time to waste."

I closed my mouth.

"Can you help me?" she demanded. Someone needed to tell her about flies, honey, and vinegar.

"What's going on?"

"It is better if you don't know."

"You want me to put you on a plane without an explanation?"

"It is a matter of life and death."

I believed her—or I believed that she believed.

"It's not my plane," I explained.

The drape-yanking, finger-snapping, put-me-on-a-plane-or-else woman deflated and tears welled her eyes. "Then I am dead."

Or at least very dramatic. Was this all just an act? A scam?

Her tears were real. I'd spent too many years watching Chariss fake tears for roles. I could tell an act when I saw one.

"I'll see what I can do to help you. Maybe I can get the plane to come back." This was just the sort of story James loved—beautiful damsel in distress, dangerous man, and James could save the day without leaving the comforts of his hotel suite.

"The plane is not here?" Her lovely face looked haggard.

"No, but I can get it here in the morning." Maybe. Hopefully. "Listen, why don't you spend the night here? I'll call James first thing. I'm sure he'd be happy to send the plane for you."

"James?"

"James Ballester."

Her eyes widened.

"He's my mother's best friend."

"The movies." She nodded as if suddenly everything was clear.

"He'll send his plane—" I hoped "—and you'll be safe. Where do you want to go?"

"Away."

"Hard to file a flight plan to away. How about Los Angeles?"

She nodded. "Yes. Los Angeles. That is fine."

"All right then. Why don't you go upstairs, pick a bedroom, and see if you can rest?"

She looked doubtfully at the stairs.

"I'll be down here and I'll call James first thing."

She nodded. Slowly. "Okay, Okay."

Marta climbed the stairs at a pace that made it seem as if her feet had been replaced by anvils. When, she turned the corner on the landing, I went back to my bedroom, stood at the doors, and watched the moonlight spill silver onto the water. What had I gotten myself into?

I slept. Badly. For a few hours. Then I tossed and turned and gave up on the idea of getting any rest.

I dragged myself out of the bed, grabbed my phone, opened the doors to the patio, and claimed a chaise. The sun hadn't yet thought about rising. It was just me, a few birds, my aching muscles, and the ocean.

It was too early to call James. Also, I wanted Marta's assurance she really wanted to leave before I called in that favor. How many times had Mia or I been adamant about something in the middle of the night only to change our minds when the sun rose? At least a hundred. Maybe more.

I shifted my gaze from the water to the notifications on my phone. The resort had tagged me on Facebook, and Twitter, and Instagram. In the pictures, Mike's arm was draped around me and we both were smiling as if we'd never had a better time. As if we were a couple. A happy couple.

Ugh.

Chariss would call as soon as she saw the photos. I knew the conversation by heart. "*What* are you doing?" she'd ask.

I'd tell her I was in Mexico at a resort—at a party.

"Fine," she'd say. "But what are you doing with your life? There's more to life than fun. When I was your age I'd—"

When she was my age, she had a hit TV show, an Emmy, an Oscar, a movie scheduled to release (her first with James), and a four-year-old daughter she saw once a year. If I was feeling snarky, I'd point out that last part.

Then she'd sigh. "I just want you to find your path."

I'd found my path and I'd chosen not to tell her about it.

Stars' children had strings pulled for them. So many strings that no matter how successful they became, they never knew if they owed their success to their own talent or to their parents' fame.

I didn't want that kind of success.

If the book I'd written sold, it would be because it was good, not because I was Poppy Fields, Chariss Carlton's wayward daughter. And if it failed, I didn't want my Emmy-winning, Oscar-winning mother to know.

The day I'd signed with an agent, Mia, Jake, and I drank champagne and toasted the book deal that was surely weeks away. That was months ago. Aside from my agent, who didn't know my real name, no one but Mia and Jake had any inkling I'd written a book.

Just Mia now.

I dropped my phone in my lap and wiped my eyes. Despite my certainty that I'd seen him last night, dawn's light told me the truth. I'd wanted to see Jake, so I'd imagined him.

I glanced at the time. Still too early to call James.

*Ding.*

A text popped up on the screen. YOU ARE IN DANGER. YOU NEED TO GO HOME.

My insides froze—heart, lungs, kidneys.

I tightened my grip on the phone. The text had come from a private number. With shaking fingers, I typed. Who is this?

YOU ARE IN DANGER!

Adrenalin flooded my system, drying my mouth and making my heart stutter. Who is this and how did you get this number?

POPPY, YOU NEED TO LEAVE. TODAY! NOW IF YOU CAN!

WHO IS THIS? Whoever they were, they weren't the only one who could type in caps.

JUST LEAVE. PLEASE.

That feeling of being watched was back. With a vengeance. In front of me was the ocean, behind me was the villa, around me were walls to ensure my privacy. No one could see me. That didn't stop me from tightening my robe around my neck.

I NEED TO KNOW YOU'RE SAFE.

My fingers flew over the keys. WHO IS THIS?

I waited for an answer. And waited.

I typed again. Slower this time. JAKE?

No answer. Nothing.

I stared at the phone.

Nothing. *Nada.*

I typed again. WHY AM I IN DANGER?

Still nothing.

I was in danger? Really?

Maybe I'd board the plane with Marta. Being sad in Los Angeles was better than being sad surrounded by happy vacationers.

Or maybe I wouldn't. Running away because of an anonymous text seemed wussy in the extreme.

JUST GO.

Not a chance. Not until you tell me who this is and why I should leave.

GO. BEFORE IT'S TOO LATE.

I dropped the phone on the chaise cushion and stood, clenching my fingers into fists. Anger replaced that initial spike of fear. Anger and annoyance. Who was sending those texts? And why?

Besides, I couldn't leave. Mia was coming.

I snatched up my phone. I'M NOT GOING ANYWHERE.

I waited for an answer, staring at the screen, silently daring whoever was typing to tell me I was in danger—again.

They answered me with silence.

A moment passed. And then another.

Nothing.

I stalked into the villa, marched into the kitchen, poured bottled water into the coffee maker, and pushed the button.

Still no response to my last text.

The coffee finished brewing and I poured myself a cup.

"Marta," I called up the stairs. "Do you want coffee?"

She didn't respond to me either.

"Marta," I called louder. "Coffee?"

Like the phone, she remained silent.

Maybe she was a deep sleeper.

I texted Mia. What time will you be here?

You're up early. Even via text, I could hear her accompanying yawn.

You wouldn't believe the morning I've had.

Is it actually morning?

Very funny. Wait till I show you the texts I just received.

From who?

Don't know. Just the thought of those texts had me clenching my jaw.

Hmm. My flight leaves at nine. See you in a few. We're having dinner with Mike.

I know. He told me. Don't you need to leave for the airport?

Yikes! TTYL.

"Marta!" If I was going to get her on a plane before Mia arrived, we needed to work fast. "Are you up?"

Silence. I poured a second cup of coffee and climbed the stairs.

Marta had chosen to sleep in the bedroom closest to the steps and there was a reason she hadn't answered my call.

Marta was dead.

# SEVEN

"Marta!" I pulled on her shoulder. *Please, God, let me be wrong.*

Marta rolled over onto her back. A residue of foam crusted her lips and her eyes were open and sightless. In her hand she clutched her phone—almost as if she'd died calling for help.

My stomach somersaulted three times—*cattawump, cattawump, cattawump*—and rejected my morning coffee. Violently. All over the tiles. My knees gave out. I thumped onto the floor hard enough to rattle my bones. *Oh. My. God.*

This couldn't be happening. Not again.

This had to be a bad dream. Except, it wasn't. Dreams don't smell like regurgitated coffee and Marta's body still lay on the bed. I crawled (I shook too hard to stand) to the landline and dialed zero.

"*Buenos días.*" The woman who answered the phone sounded as bright and hopeful as a sunrise.

"I…" there wasn't enough air in my lungs. I inhaled through my mouth. "I…"

"*Cómo puedo ayudarle?*" Concern colored her voice.

"I…" I clamped my hand over my lips, covering a second wave of nausea.

"*Está bien?*" She sounded worried now.

No. I was not *bien*. There was a corpse staring at me and I couldn't breathe. "Please, send help." The three words emptied my lungs.

"*Qué pasa?*"

So many things. I forced more air into my lungs. "This is Poppy Fields. Marta Vargas is dead in the extra bedroom."

"*Que?*"

"She's dead. Dea..." My voice broke. What was the right word? Muerte? "*Marta Vargas es muerta.*"

Apparently my awful Spanish was good enough. The operator gasped.

"Please, send someone. Please hurry."

"*Sí, señora.*"

"*Gracias.*"

I hung up the phone and curled into a fetal position on the floor.

This was bad. So, so, so bad. Marta Vargas (poor Marta) was the second body I'd found in a matter of five weeks. The police called that a pattern.

I hauled myself off the floor and stumbled to the steps. Clutching the bannister like a life-preserver, I tripped down the stairs and opened the front door.

Then I retreated to the steps. I sank onto the third stair and waited for help. *Déjà vu*—especially when it came to bodies— was a terrible thing.

"Miss Fields? Señorita Fields?"

"In here."

Two men wearing poplin suits pushed through the open front door and stepped inside.

A dapper man regarded my stained nightgown with distaste. "Miss Fields?"

"Yes."

"I am Carlos Silva. I manage the resort. This—" he waved his hand at the other man "—is Oscar Valdez, head of security."

I nodded mutely—saying *pleased to meet you* seemed wrong. Plus, the air wasn't mixing properly in my lungs and little stars were dancing around me.

"You told the receptionist that Marta Vargas was dead in your villa."

I nodded.

"Where is the body?"

"Upstairs."

Valdez slipped past me and climbed the stairs.

"You're sure it's Miss Vargas?" Señor Silva wrung his hands. "You're sure she's dead?"

I stood. "I am."

"What happened?"

Standing had been a mistake. I sank onto the couch (sitting helped with the stars), told Señor Silva about Marta's unexpected arrival at the villa, and repeated every word she'd said to me.

"Did she tell you the man's name?" Señor Valdez stood on the stairs and mopped his forehead with a handkerchief.

"I assumed it was Javier. I saw them together yesterday."

"Javier Diaz?" Valdez looked positively green.

So did Silva.

Asparagus green.

"Who is Javier Diaz?"

Neither man answered. They just exchanged a look. With each other. I was on the outside looking in.

"Who is he?" I insisted.

"He *might* be a senior executive in the Sinaloa organization." Señor Silva's voice was hardly a whisper and the green of his skin had morphed from asparagus to avocado.

Valdez grimaced and wiped his brow again.

"You mean a drug lord with the Sinaloa Cartel?" Oh. Hell. "You have to call the police."

Whatever shade was greener than avocado—that was the shade Silva and Diaz turned next.

I too was feeling green. I'd shared a pool deck with a drug lord. I'd shared a drink with a drug lord. Those men with the bellies and the mustaches and the tattoos—they were probably *sicarios*. Killers. And there was a dead woman in my upstairs bedroom. A woman who had stormed away from them. A two-year-old could make the connection. I glared at Silva. "You invited a drug lord to your grand opening?"

"No." Silva held up his hands as if he were warding off evil. "I didn't invite Diaz. He informed me he was coming."

"And you let him?"

"One doesn't say no to Javier Diaz."

I had.

And now there was a dead woman in my villa.

And the two men in front of me didn't seem to have a plan for removing her.

"Someone needs to call the police. Now."

Looking very much as if he'd rather chew off his arm, Valdez pulled a phone out of his jacket pocket and dialed.

Twenty minutes later, another man in another poplin suit arrived. He regarded me with the exact same mixture of suspicion and derision as Detective Parks had. "Detective Gonzales." He flashed a badge.

I seriously hoped Detectives Parks and Gonzales never met.

"Where is the body?" Gonzales demanded.

"I'll show you." Señor Valdez waved toward the stairs.

"In a minute." Detective Gonzales returned his gaze to me. "Who are you?"

"Poppy Fields."

His eyes narrowed. "Your real name."

"That is my real name." Chariss had an unfortunate sense of humor. That, or she never imagined naming me after the source of heroin would be a problem. Maybe both. Probably both.

He snorted. "Tell me what happened."

I told Detective Gonzales everything I'd told Señor Silva.

Unlike Silva and Valdez, the mention of Javier Diaz didn't make Gonzales's skin turn green. The detective's eyes lit up. His nose twitched. Beneath his twitching nose, his mustache twitched. His lips curled into a predatory grin.

"So, she was afraid of Javier Diaz? You're sure?"

"No. I'm not. She never said the man's name. But as I told these men, I saw them together and assumed they were a couple or he wanted them to be."

"Señorita Vargas was Señor Diaz's guest at the resort," offered Silva.

Detective Gonzales stroked his upper lip with a knuckle and stared at me. "And you didn't know her?"

"No."

"You let a woman you didn't know spend the night in your villa?" Disbelief colored the detective's voice.

Of course I'd let her stay. Her grandmother had been kind to my mother. I didn't tell him that. "She was afraid—terrified —and there were fresh bruises on her arm."

"You didn't know her? Not at all?" The man was like a dog with a bone.

"I met her yesterday."

Gonzales's predatory grin grew more predatory. "Yester-day? Are you sure?"

"Positive."

The unpleasant smile curling his lips sent shivers down my spine.

He pulled out his cellphone and shoved the screen under my nose. There was a picture of Marta and me smiling at each other as if we'd been best friends since we were old enough to toddle. As if we'd never had such a wonderful time. As if we planned on toasting each other's weddings, sending extrava-gant baby gifts, drinking wine together every Tuesday, and taking girls trips every February. "You still don't know her?"

I shrugged. "That was a photo op."

"Looks to me like you're friends. Good friends."

"No."

"We'll see." His eyes narrowed to slits. "May I see your passport, Miss Fields?" He pronounced my name as if he didn't yet believe anyone would name their child Poppy Fields. Right then, I didn't believe it either.

"Of course." I stood, crossed the room to the door of the master bedroom, and paused. "Señor Silva will vouch for me."

Gonzales raised an eyebrow. "You just said Señor Silva welcomed the head of a drug cartel into his hotel. You'll forgive me if I don't take his word."

When he put it that way, I couldn't argue.

I glanced at Silva—his skin tone was greener than ever.

Without another word, I slipped into the bedroom, opened the wall safe, and grabbed my passport.

"Here it is." I walked toward the detective with my passport held out.

He took it from me, opened the cover, read my name, then slipped the document into the inside pocket of his suit.

"What are you doing?" I demanded.

"You will remain in Mexico."

Could he even do that? I directed my gaze at Silva whose skin had passed from green to gray. He was no help.

"You are a material witness in a murder investigation," declared Detective Gonzales. "You will not leave the country. This—" he patted his coat pocket "—is my way of making sure you don't."

We'd just see about that. I'd have my passport back within twenty-four hours or the lawyers at Gardner, Jackson & Bray would eat their fee. A thing that never happened. Ever.

Detective Gonzales might be scary and Javier Diaz might be dangerous but they had nothing on Chariss's lawyers. They were barracudas posing as humans. Compared to the senior partners at Gardner, Jackson & Bray, the detective and the drug lord looked like little girls with a lemonade stand.

"May I have one of your cards, Detective?"

He dug one out of a leather case and I snatched it from his fingers.

"You will not leave the country," he repeated.

I refrained—barely—from telling him I'd heard him the first time.

*Brnng, brnng.*

Señor Silva patted his coat pockets, pulled out a phone, and frowned at the screen. "*Si?*"

The resort manager listened to the caller and his skin color took a turn for the worse. Zombie-apocalypse worse. "*Eso es horrible.*" That I understood. The rest of his responses were so rapid, I only caught one word—*muerte.*

Someone else was dead.

He hung up the phone and looked at Detective Gonzales. "*Vámonos!*"

They were leaving? There was a body upstairs. "You can't leave!"

"There's been a murder." Señor Silva winced as if he'd said too much. "Please, Miss Fields, don't talk to anyone."

The two men exchanged a few words so rapidly I caught none of what they said. Then they hurried toward the door.

"Wait!" Their steps paused at my panicked voice. "What about Marta?'

"An overdose, yes?" asked Detective Gonzales.

"Sí," replied Señor Valdez.

"I'll send a couple of uniforms to deal with it." Detective Gonzales turned his back on us.

"It" not her. I was going to enjoy setting Gardner, Jackson & Bray loose on the detective.

"Señor Silva!" My voice slowed the two men's steps a second time.

The resort manager's hands clenched, his shoulders

hunched, and he looked over his shoulder, annoyance writ clearly on his face. "What?"

"Since Detective Gonzales insists that I stay in Mexico, I'll need a new villa."

He winced.

"You cannot expect me to stay here. It's a crime scene." Not to mention, there was no way Mia would stay upstairs by herself—not when someone had just died up there.

With a resigned shrug, Silva nodded. "I will get you another villa, Señorita, do not worry."

Silva and Gonzales hurried out the door.

I picked up a Jo Malone English pear and freesia travel candle and a framed picture of Mia and me taken at Palmyra Peak in Telluride and deposited them on the dining table. I added a second picture—Chariss and me at the Oscars—and the cashmere throw I'd draped over the back of the couch.

Chariss never traveled without a suitcase full of photographs, candles, throws, monogrammed coffee mugs, and her own pillows. When she was on an extended shoot, she brought her own sheets.

Making a hotel feel like home was one of her habits I'd acquired through osmosis.

"What are you doing?" Mia stood in the doorway.

I'd never been so glad to see anyone. My knees shook with relief. "I'm packing."

"Why? I just got here."

"We're getting a new villa."

"What's wrong with this one?"

"Someone died upstairs."

She didn't respond right away—it's hard to talk with your mouth hanging open. Finally, she snapped her jaw shut. "What?"

"I let someone spend the night here and she died."

"Died?"

"Yes."

She stepped inside the villa and André took her spot in the doorway. "Did I hear you say someone died in your villa?" He opened his arms as if he could tell I needed a hug.

I rushed into his embrace. "I didn't know you were coming."

"Mia wanted to surprise you. Who died?"

"Marta Vargas."

"Who?" asked Mia.

"A Mexican movie star." My response was muffled by André's shirt.

"She did a bunch of telenovelas then moved on to film. Big star." André probably knew precisely how much she could have earned per Instagram post.

"And you knew her?" Mia demanded.

"I didn't know her. I met her yesterday."

"And she died *here* last night?" My best friend sounded as suspicious as Detective Gonzales. "What was she doing here?"

"She showed up here terrified. She was certain someone was going to kill her. She wanted me to get her out of Mexico."

"What happened to her?" asked Mia.

"She overdosed."

Mia leveled a squinty look my way. The look said many things. *Holy hell!* and *Do the police know this is your second body?* and *Should I be worried?*

I pulled loose of André's arms. "If you'll finish gathering things in here, I'll pack my clothes.

"Why don't we just go home?" asked André.

"I can't. The police took my passport."

"They what?" Mia's screech was loud enough to bring Señor Valdez to the top of the stairs.

I held up my hands and tilted my head toward the man who'd be removing Marta. "We're fine. I'm just packing."

"They what?" Mia's voice lowered to a furious whisper.

"The detective took my passport."

"Can he do that? Where is this detective?" Mia was a firm believer that power, influence and money could solve any problem. She had plenty of all three.

"He left."

"With your passport?" Already she was scrolling through her contacts looking for someone who could fix the problem.

"I'm calling Ruth Gardner."

Mia looked up from her phone. If a named partner at Gardner, Jackson & Bray couldn't get my passport returned (with an apology and a bottle of Cristal for my trouble) no one could. "Where did this detective go?" she demanded.

"To investigate a murder."

This time both my friends' jaws dropped.

André recovered first. "What murder?"

"No idea. I think it happened at the main hotel since the resort manager went with him."

Mia wheeled on André. "What kind of place did you book her into?"

"It's not André's fault."

Mia glanced at the stairs then whispered, "Do they know about Jake?"

"No. And I'd like to keep it that way."

# EIGHT

We moved into a villa three doors down. Same wall of glass. Same pool. Same chaises on the patio. No dead body.

That part was an improvement.

"In there." I directed the bellman to the first-floor bedroom then held up my phone and turned to face my friends. "I'm going to call the lawyer."

They both nodded, their expressions grim.

I stepped out on the patio, found the law firm's number in my contacts, and dialed.

"Gardner, Wilson & Bray," said a voice in Los Angeles.

"This is Poppy Fields calling for Ruth Gardner."

"Is Miss Gardner expecting your call?"

"No," I replied, sinking onto a sun-drenched chaise. "But I have an emergency."

"Please hold."

André and Mia spilled out onto the patio.

"Which room did Marta Vargas die in?" Mia's gauzy maxi-dress ruffled in the breeze. So did her flowing hair. She looked like a wind sprite or a white witch or Stevie Nicks.

"The one at the top of the stairs."

"That settles it." Mia turned her attention to André. "I'm taking the other one."

"Don't take any drugs and you should both be fine."

"She really overdosed?" Mia eased onto the second chaise and stretched out her already perfectly tanned legs.

"Yes."

"On what?"

"I'm not sure but I'm guessing Venti."

"Venti? Seriously?"

"The policeman in Los Angeles, Detective Parks, told me how dangerous it is."

André paled. "People are dying from Venti? That's supposed to be a party drug."

"People die from Molly," I replied.

"Not often."

I wasn't up for an argument about the stupidity of ingesting foreign substances with questionable histories so I shrugged. "You know what I know. Please, don't take any of that stuff, okay?"

"Miss Fields?" the receptionist in Los Angeles had the most professional voice on earth. Its tone said there were many important things to be accomplished.

"I'm here."

"Ms. Gardner is in a meeting." Now her voice was apologetic. "May she call you when she's free?" Ruth Gardner was never free. Our call would cost hundreds of dollars.

"Yes. Do you need my number?"

"Should she call you at the number you're calling from?"

"Yes. Thank you." I hung up and dropped the phone in my lap.

"What did they say?" asked Mia.

"Ruth will call me back."

"You're on a first name basis with Ruth Gardner?" André wasn't easily impressed but apparently calling Ruth Gardner by her first name had moved me up a few pegs. His expression was awed.

"The firm handles everything for Chariss."

Mia yawned. "They handle everything for my dad too but we're not on a first-name basis."

"When Dad disappeared, they took care of things." I looked out at the waves, avoiding my friends' gazes. "And, two years ago, when Chariss had Dad declared dead—" against my wishes "—we spent a lot of time together."

"They sued my father." André's father's epic flop had left half of Hollywood in cover-their-ass mode. There had been lawsuits. So many lawsuits. And André had gone from being the most popular guy in school to a pariah only fit to be friends with the new girls—namely Mia and me. He pulled a chair out from under the pergola and angled it toward the sun. "So, what happened yesterday?"

I told them about the scene at the pool. I told them about the party. I told them about Javier.

"I can't believe there's a drug lord staying here." Mia's whisper was raspy and she glanced over her shoulder as if she expected to see a hired killer. "Didn't you vet this place at all?" The second question she directed to André.

"Of course I did."

"*Hmpph.*" She wasn't buying it.

"It's not like André can control who else stays here."

"Thank you, Poppy." André offered me the sweetest of smiles then shifted his gaze to Mia. "If there's a super-villain on the property, maybe there's a James Bond type here, too." André knew Mia had a killer crush on Daniel Craig.

"You think?" Mia sounded marginally less miffed.

"Anything's possible." What were the odds of me finding two bodies? Those odds had to be astronomical but I'd still found them.

We sat in silence—pondering possibilities—for three

whole minutes before Mia said, "I'm hungry. Are you hungry?"

I pictured Marta's sightless eyes and shook my head.

"I could eat," said André.

"You can always eat. It's not fair." Mia stuck out her tongue. She didn't have much room to talk. She was the approximate size of a toothpick.

"It's not my fault I've got an awesome metabolism." If André ever got tired of being an agent to the newly famous, he could model. He might even make more money.

"I need to stay here for my call." I pointed at the phone. "There's an *al fresco* café up at the hotel."

"Don't be ridiculous. We're not leaving you." Mia shielded her face from the sun with her forearm. "We'll call for room service."

Mia wandered inside and picked up the landline. She ordered a breaded chicken breast stuffed with goat cheese and mushrooms topped with chipotle cream.

She stood in the doorway and waved at us. "What do you want?"

"Ceviche, please." André planted a hand on his hip. "I swear, lately every calorie I eat is worth ten." Our cue to tell him how amazing he looked.

Instead, Mia rolled her eyes. "You already told us about your metabolism—we know you're fishing for compliments, and frankly, your head shouldn't get any bigger." She shifted her gaze my way. "What do you want?" Her tone made it clear she expected me to eat.

André pursed his lips. "You should eat something."

Two against one. I ceded. "Maybe grilled shrimp."

With a satisfied nod, Mia ordered the ceviche and the shrimp then reclaimed her chaise.

"So, what's the plan?" André stared out at the ocean. "Are we out of here as soon as you get your passport back?"

"Let's see how quickly that happens." Even with Gardner,

Wilson & Bray on my side, my hopes for leaving in the next day or so weren't high.

"I want to hear about those mysterious texts," said Mia.

André turned his gaze from the ocean to me and his brows rose. "What mysterious texts?"

With Marta's death, I'd forgotten all about the texts. I handed Mia my phone and she read the stream. "Jake?"

"Long story." Or wishful thinking. "I thought I saw him last night."

Mia got up off her chaise, joined me on mine, and hugged me. "You're having a hard time with his death, aren't you?"

A lump lodged itself in my throat.

"We're stuck here and that's not exactly ideal but I'm going to cheer you up." She squeezed my shoulders. "I promise."

I didn't argue but I had my doubts.

*Brnng, brnng.*

Our heads swiveled toward the villa and I rose.

*Brnng, brnng.*

I hurried inside and grabbed the receiver. "Hello."

"Miss Fields?"

"Yes."

"It's Carols Silva. We met earlier. Do you remember me?"

The resort manager. How could I forget? "Did you get my passport back?"

He cleared his throat. "No. I'm calling about Irene Vargas."

"What about Irene?"

"She wants to see you."

My heart sank to my ankles. I had to tell that lovely older woman about how her granddaughter died? "Oh?"

"Please come up to the hotel, we have a car waiting for you."

"A car?"

"To take you to the hospital."

"The hospital?"

"I thought you heard me when I was on the phone at your villa. Someone broke into the Vargas's room and beat them. Badly. Señor Vargas is dead and Señora Vargas is in critical condition."

I searched for words.

"She may not have much time."

"I'm on my way." I hung up the phone.

"What's going on?" André asked from the doorway to the patio.

"Someone murdered Marta's grandfather and her grandmother may die. She wants to see me."

"Now? We just ordered lunch."

I stared at him.

André winced. "That came out wrong."

It sure had.

"What I meant was this day has been one crisis after another. You need to take care of you."

"Later."

"Then I'm coming with you."

I shook my head. "You have ceviche coming."

"Mia can eat it. And your shrimp. Or she can put them in the fridge and we'll eat them later."

I walked up to him and kissed his cheek. "Thanks, but you know Mia. She hates to eat alone." Then I called out to the patio. "Mia, I'm going to see Marta Vargas's grandmother. I'll be back in a little while."

"What about lunch?" she replied.

"Save it for me."

I hurried into my bedroom, dug through my hastily repacked suitcases, found a straw clutch, and jammed my phone and the villa's key inside. Then I slipped my bare feet into a pair of sandals and called to Mia and André, "I'm leaving. I'll call you."

True to his word, Señor Silva had a car waiting for me.

The driver took me to a small hospital where a nurse led me to a bed cordoned off by curtains. Multiple monitors beeped every few seconds.

Just yesterday, Irene Vargas had been healthy and strong. Now she looked tiny and weak.

The parts of her face that weren't covered with bandages were purple with bruises. Her left wrist was in a cast and tubes ran into her right arm. Tears leaked from her eyes and ran down her cheeks.

Who would do such a thing?

"Señora Vargas. Irene. It's me, Poppy Fields." I took the chair on the right side of the bed and gently clasped her fingers. Her skin felt papery thin and I imagined I was holding bones.

Slowly, Irene turned her head in my direction.

"You came." She regarded me through eyes so swollen it was a wonder she could see me.

"Of course."

"Daniel is dead." Her voice, barely a whisper, carried more sadness than was possible for a woman to bear.

I tightened my grip on her fingers. "I'm so sorry."

"And Marta too."

I nodded and my eyes filled with tears.

"These men that Marta got mixed up with." Irene closed her eyes but the tears kept coming. "They are ruthless."

I knew that. The beaten-near-to-death grandmother in the bed in front of me was all the evidence I needed.

"Marta got caught in the middle." Her fingers stiffened. "Did she give it to you?"

"Marta didn't give me anything."

"They will think you have it."

Fear crept across the antiseptic white floor tiles and wrapped around my ankles. "Have what? And who is they?"

"The Cartel—" she paused and her face tightened as if one of her wounds especially pained her "—and Mérida."

I'd heard about Mexican cartels—everyone had—but who or what was Mérida? The fear slinked past my ankles, climbed over my knees, and coiled in my stomach. "What are they looking for?"

"They will think Marta gave it to you. You must get out of Mexico. Today."

Easier said than done without a passport. "What does everyone think Marta gave me?"

"You need to run."

"The police took my passport."

The few visible parts of Irene that weren't bruised paled. "I am so sorry my family brought you into this. You must rent a boat and sail up the coast. Do something. Get out." Her fingers within the confines of my hand turned ice cold.

"Irene, you need to rest."

She replied with a miniscule jerk of her chin. "Marta thought she could outsmart them." She turned her head away and a sob shook her fractured body. When she looked back at me, her face was wet with fresh tears. "Did she look peaceful?"

"She did," I lied.

Something like a smile flitted across Irene's battered face and she squeezed my hand. "You are a terrible actress."

I'd heard that before. More than once.

*Beeeeep.* One of the machines went crazy.

The nurse who'd led me to Irene rushed into the tiny space and pushed me out of the way. Two more nurses joined her.

I let go of Irene's fingers and retreated to the hallway.

*Beeeeep.*

There was a spate of rapid fire directions and then silence.

I didn't need to speak Spanish to understand what had happened. Irene Vargas was dead.

# NINE

I returned to an empty villa. Empty except for a note that said, *We're going parasailing Back by five.*

So much for *being there* for me.

I glanced at my phone. One o'clock.

The villa's emptiness swirled around me like a killing fog. My throat tightened and tears gathered on my lashes. I'd watched a woman die, held her hand as she passed away.

Loneliness, which had been sneaking around since my arrival, plonked down on the couch, put its feet on the coffee table, and asked for a beer.

Nope. No way. No how. I refused to sit around the villa alone.

Also, my stomach was making grumbly noises

I walked up to the hotel and found a table at the patio restaurant. The waiter magically appeared with chips, salsa, and guacamole. Ordering a margarita was oh-so tempting but day-drinking alone seemed more pathetic than hanging out in my villa by myself.

I ordered mineral water and fish tacos.

"May I get you anything else?" he asked.

"Poppy! Are you here by yourself? May I join you?" Brett

Cannon pulled out a chair before I could reply. "Those look good." He jerked his chin toward the basket of tortilla chips then shifted his gaze to the waiter. *"Modelo, por favor."* His Spanish sounded worse than mine.

I'd come to the patio to escape loneliness. Loneliness might have made me cry or hogged the remote but it wouldn't have annoyed me half to death.

He stretched his legs out underneath the table, leaned back, and laced his fingers behind his neck. "I heard through the grapevine that you had some excitement."

Excitement? Not the adjective I'd use. "A woman died."

Brett helped himself to a chip and dipped it into my guacamole. "I heard she overdosed."

"You're very well informed."

"Looking out for my investor's interests."

"Did you also hear that the police have taken my passport? I'm pissed. My mother will be furious." Chariss wouldn't care except for the legal bill. "James Ballester will be apoplectic. Can you imagine the publicity we could generate?" I squared my fingers like a view-finder. "I can just see the headlines. Heck, I could write the copy. *Poppy Fields, daughter of Hollywood star Chariss Carlton, was detained in Mexico while staying at—*"

"Stop."

I kept going. "Ms. Fields only crime seems to have been taking pity on a woman being victimized by a member of the Sinaloa drug cartel. The cartel member was also staying at—"

Brett choked on his chip.

"How about this? Ms. Fields was staying at the same resort where international star Marta Vargas died of an overdose—"

"Stop!"

I did not like Brett. Plus, his attitude about Marta's death bothered me. Also, he was eating my chips. Without asking. I kept going. "In a related story, Marta Vargas' grandparents,

Irene and Daniel Vargas, were found murdered at the same resort—"

Brett looked around as if worried someone would hear me. "Shhh!"

The waiter deposited three perfect tacos in front of me and a beer in front of Brett. "May I get you anything else?"

"No, thank you," I replied.

"Anything for you, sir?"

Brett tipped his head and drank from the bottle. "Another beer."

When the waiter moved on to another table, Brett shifted in his chair and leaned toward me. "Look, I'll see what the resort can do about getting your passport returned."

I didn't hold out much hope that the resort would do anything. "I called my lawyer."

"Your lawyer?"

"Ruth Gardner with Gardner, Wilson & Bray."

Brett paled.

I glanced at the time on my cell. "In fact, Ruth is due to call me in a few minutes."

"You left early last night." Brett's changing the subject wouldn't change the situation. "You missed a great party."

"I dealt with the aftermath."

Brett coughed. Hard. As if the beer had gone down the wrong pipe in his throat. He tapped his palm against his chest. "Any idea what drug Marta Vargas took?"

"No." I returned my second taco to the plate. I'd lost my appetite.

"Such a shame." He shook his head. "She was a great actress."

It was doubtful Brett had ever watched a telenovela or seen a Mexican film.

Active dislike for the man at my table swept through me. "How is the resort going to handle the PR of an overdose and two murders in its opening week?"

A cloud settled on Brett's face. "The reporters have better stories. We'll keep it quiet."

Three people were dead. Did he really think he could keep murder quiet in the age of instant news? "There are hundreds of people here."

"And very few of them know what happened."

My phone rang.

"*Jaws?*" asked Brett.

"The ringtone? I thought it was perfect for a lawyer." I picked up my cell. "I've got to take this."

Brett tilted his face toward the sun. "I don't mind."

I did mind. I pushed out of my chair and walked away, pausing at a low wall where I perched and stared out at the water. "Ruth?"

"Poppy," she replied. "What happened?" Ruth didn't waste her clients' time or money with niceties like asking after their health or family.

"I'm in Mexico and the police have taken my passport."

The scratch of her pencil on a legal pad carried through the phone line. "Why?"

"An actress named Marta Vargas overdosed in my villa."

"Did you provide her drugs?"

"No." If anyone else asked me that I'd be offended but Ruth was being thorough. "I let her spend the night because she appeared to be afraid of her boyfriend. When I went to wake her this morning, I found her dead."

"Doesn't sound like too much of a problem." More scratches on the pad. "What's the police detective's name?

"Hector Gonzales. I've got all his information back at the villa."

"I'll call you if I need it. Anything else?"

I looked around, making sure no one could hear me. "Just so you know, not long ago, I found my boyfriend dead of an overdose.

After a near-endless silence, Ruth asked, "What was his name?"

"Jake."

"Last name?" A hint of impatience crept into her voice.

"Smith," I supplied.

"What did he do for a living?"

"Something with the music industry."

"Can you be more specific?"

"No." I glanced over at my table where Brett was polishing off my chips and eyeing my remaining tacos. "I never really knew."

"Okay. Let me get to work on this. If I get your passport, how quickly can you get out of Mexico?"

"James Ballester is down here. In La Paz. He said I could borrow his plane whenever I needed it."

"Good." The staccato beat of her pencil tapping against the pad was so loud it almost seemed as if I sat across a desk from her. "Ask him to keep it ready."

"Okay."

"I'll call you later." She hung up without a goodbye.

The to-do list was short. Call James. But, as wonderful as James was, he wouldn't (couldn't) keep a secret from Chariss. If I told him what had happened since I arrived, Chariss would know within an hour. I could hear her now, "*You've come up with a whole new genre, Poppy. Screwball-tragedies.*"

I looked back at my table. Brett was eating one of my tacos. I didn't care. My appetite was completely gone and I was due to have dinner with Mia, André, and Mike in a few hours anyway. I waved at Brett, made an apologetic face, and pointed at the phone. Hopefully he'd think my call was so important I had to forego his company.

I followed the soapbush-lined path back to the villa, stopping to smell jasmine being trained up trellises. The resort really had spent a fortune on landscaping.

If the sunscreen, sunglasses, lip balm, and damp towels

strewn around the living room were any indication, Mia and
André had returned. "Hello," I called.

"Shhh." André's head popped up from the couch. "Mia's
taking a nap."

André was stretched out on the sofa as if he thought Mia
had the right idea. I shoved his feet out of the way and
sat down.

He eyed me critically. "You look pale."

"I feel pale."

"How did things go with Marta's grandmother?"

"She died." Somewhere inside me tears and sobs and real
sadness waited, but I was too overwhelmed to feel.

André sat up, draped an arm around my shoulders, and
pressed my head against his chest. "I'm so sorry."

"Someone beat her." I covered my mouth with my palm. I
couldn't tell him. I couldn't explain the bruises or the blood or
the swelling or her pain. "When she died, I was holding
her hand."

"Do you want to skip dinner and stay home tonight?"

"More than anything." Longing crept into my voice. "Do
you think Mia would consider cancelling?"

"On Mike? No."

"But—"

"Remember Operation Cheer Up Poppy?"

"Ugh."

"I'll see if she'll go without us. And if she won't, maybe
we can arrange for dinner here."

Which meant a night of watching Mike and Mia casting
bedroom eyes at each other with no way to escape. "That
sounds good in theory but—"

"But the Mia and Mike show?"

"Yeah." Mia and Mike. Friends with benefits. A mutual
admiration society of two. They could be a tad wearing.

"I'll go to dinner. It's not worth the argument. But, I'm not going dancing. Will you come back here with me after we eat?" I asked.

"And deprive myself hours of watching Mia and Mike do everything but the nasty on the dance floor?" He leaned forward and kissed my cheek.

---

MIA FLOATED into my room on a dawn-hued cloud of printed silk and plopped onto the bed. "What are you wearing tonight?"

"I don't know."

"Well figure it out. Our reservation is in thirty minutes."

"I—"

"Don't think for a minute you're getting out of dinner. There is no way I'm going to let you sit here all night and brood."

"Yes, ma'am." My voice was meek. Sometimes it was easier to go along than to argue. Especially when the point of contention was just dinner. "I thought I'd wear that cutaway maxi T-shirt with the wide leg pants."

She sniffed. "Isn't that black?"

"It is."

"Don't you think you need a little color?"

"Not tonight."

She opened her mouth as if she meant to argue but shrugged instead. "I'll let you get ready."

When I emerged from the bathroom, an emerald green minaudiere lay on the bed.

Mia—even when you thought she'd ceded your point—she kept trying.

I pulled a black Dries Van Noten envelope clutch out of my suitcase and slipped my phone, a lipstick, and the room card inside. I returned the little bag to her room then joined Mia and André on the patio.

Dinner wasn't so bad. The maître d' led us to an intimate table for four on a fairy-lit veranda. We shared a pitcher of margaritas then ordered. When it came, the food was totally phenomenal. Best of all, I was with three people who could carry a conversation without me. I said not a word.

Until Mike turned to me and asked, "What happened last night? Did you ever find Jake?"

"Jake?" Mia's perfect eyebrows rose into perfect arches.

I shrugged. "I saw someone who looked just like him."

"You mean he's not here?" Mike lifted the salted rim of a margarita glass to his lips. "Too bad. I wanted to meet him."

Mia's mouth tightened and I shifted my gaze to my lap. Loneliness was back and he'd brought his friend, Sadness.

Mike reached out and squeezed my arm. "I didn't mean to upset you."

"It's just—" it wasn't Mike's fault that people around me were dropping like flies. "I'm not—"

"They broke up." Mia nodded "It was ugly. Let's talk about something else."

"Wait." A fearsome expression settled onto Mike's face. "Is he stalking you? Is that why you thought you saw him?"

"No. He's not a stalker." He was a corpse.

Mia picked up her glass. "Seriously, let's talk about something else."

Mike donned a what's-a-guy-supposed-to-do expression and shifted his attention to André. "Did you hear someone was murdered in the hotel?

As topics went, that one wasn't any better.

"We heard," said André. "Hey, I've been meaning to tell you, I saw you in *Singapore Sling*. You were awesome."

André was a genius. There was nothing actors liked better than hearing how marvelous they'd been in their most recent project. Mike had played an American drug dealer who got killed before the halfway mark.

"It was a good project." Mike nodded sagely. "Good director."

"So, what's next for you?"

"Acting might not be my thing."

Mike was the only one of us who'd chosen to follow in his famous parent's footsteps. Mia didn't sing, I didn't act, and André broke out in hives at the mere mention of producing a movie.

"Oh?" Mia sounded surprised.

"Investing might be more my style." He sipped his margarita. "When we were shooting in Asia, I met a group of investors who are looking for opportunities."

"Like the tequila company," I ventured.

"Exactly."

"What have you decided about that?" I lifted my glass to my lips.

"Investing in companies in Mexico isn't the smartest move right now."

Mia tilted her head like a curious robin. "Oh?"

"Too much unrest. Too much violence."

I wasn't about to argue.

"So what are you thinking?" she asked.

Mike answered her with a cagey smile. "Still looking for the right opportunity." His gaze slid from Mia to me. "You have an admirer."

"I do?"

"That guy over there. He's been staring at you all night."

As one, our heads swiveled.

"Subtle," Mike muttered.

I didn't care about subtlety. Not when Javier Diaz was staring at me like I was the most delicious thing on the menu.

# TEN

"Who is that?" Mike jerked his chin toward Javier.

According to the detective who'd taken my passport, Javier Diaz was a leader in the Sinaloa Cartel. But if that was true, why hadn't he been arrested? Why was he lounging on the patio looking as if he owned the place? "Nobody."

"He doesn't look like a nobody."

Mike was right. Even in a loose linen shirt, khakis, and a pair of espadrilles, Javier Diaz looked like someone who usually wore bespoke suits. And that was if one didn't notice the Vacheron Constantin Tour de l'Ile on his wrist. The watch cost more than a million dollars and was a status symbol for the super-rich. I'd only seen three before tonight. One on the wrist of a Saudi prince. One had belonged to André's father (before the flop and the lawsuits). And one was James Ballester's pride and joy.

"Nice watch." André recognized it too.

"Who is he?" Mike insisted.

"His name is Javier Diaz."

"But who is he?" Translation—what did Javier do to afford a watch like that?

I leaned forward and pitched my voice low. "He's a leader in the Sinaloa Cartel."

"Well, that explains the watch."

"You mean like a cartel cartel? Headless people in Juarez cartel?" Mike's cheeks had paled.

"Exactly. He's dangerous. Stop staring at him."

As one, we swiveled our gazes away.

"Like I said—" Mike shook his head "—subtlety isn't your thing."

"What I don't understand is how he can just wander around the resort." Mia whispered so quietly we all leaned in to hear her. "Can't the police arrest him?"

"I think they need proof." I was pretty sure if Detective Gonzales could prove Javier was a drug lord, he'd be in jail. That, or Javier had paid off all the right people.

Mike snuck another look at Javier. "He seems really into you, Poppy."

I shuddered. People who got mixed up with drug cartels ended up dead in unpleasant ways. An image of Irene's battered face flashed in front of my eyes. "Not in a million years."

"Just ignore him," said Mia "He'll get the idea."

I sincerely doubted that.

A waiter cleared our plates.

"Does anyone want another drink?" Mike glanced at his Rolex (not remotely impressive when compared to the time-piece on Javier's wrist). "The club doesn't open until ten."

"You guys go ahead," I said. "I'm heading back. It's been a rough day."

Mia's lower lip extended in a pout. "We're going dancing. It won't be as much fun without you." Her eyes narrowed. "And I'm not sure it's such a good idea that you be alone."

"Maybe tomorrow tonight." Assuming my passport wasn't returned. If—when—

I reclaimed that blessed blue-clad document, I'd be out of

Mexico within minutes. "Right now, I feel as if I've been run over by a truck."

"I'll go back to the villa with you," offered André. "All that parasailing wore me out."

"It's early," Mia argued. "You should come out for a little while. It will cheer you up."

Cheer me up? Not likely. "It's been a long day." The understatement of all understatements. "Besides, you and Mike will do just fine without us." If she thought I'd missed them rubbing their knees together under the tables, she was wrong.

I stood.

So did André.

So did Mike, who dropped a goodnight kiss on my cheek.

André closed his hand on my elbow and together we wound our way through the tables. We stopped at the edge of the patio and admired the starlit water.

"I'm sorry I got you into this mess," he said. "It was my idea for you to come here."

"It's not your fault."

"I convinced you to come."

"I didn't need much convincing. Besides, this trouble is nothing a good lawyer and a private plane can't fix. I have both."

"You have a private plane?"

"If I need one, James will send me his Gulfstream in a heartbeat."

We stepped onto the pathway that led to the private villas.

"Are you okay in those shoes?"

I wore the same Louboutin stilettos I'd worn last night. "I'm fine."

"It's at least half a mile walk."

"I'll be fine. Just don't make me run."

We strolled.

"So, what's up with you and Cody?" I asked.

André shook his head. "Let's not go there."

"You know all my drama."

"He..." André paused and looked out at the ocean, his face suddenly sad. "We want different things."

I took his hand in mine. "You'll meet the right man someday."

"So will you."

"Until then we've got each other." I pulled on his arm. "Come on, I want to get out of these clothes."

"You are looking very chic for a beach resort."

I snorted. "Let's go."

The sounds from the restaurant faded, replaced by the lap of waves on the beach.

The lights faded too.

We walked in the near dark with the scent of jasmine hanging over us like a heavenly cloud. So different from last night when I'd feared someone was following me.

André stumbled. "You'd think they'd—"

"*Eeek!*"

"What—" André turned toward me. Horror registered on his face and he brought his hands to his cheeks. "Oh my God. Oh my God."

The man who held the knife at my throat tightened his grip on my arm.

"What do you want?" I rasped. Leaning away from the knife pressed beneath my jaw meant leaning into the man holding me.

"She gave it to you."

"Who?" I swallowed, hyper-aware of the knife's blade on my neck. "What?"

"*Dónde está?*"

"Where is what?"

"You want money? I've got money." André reached inside his linen jacket.

The man's hold on me became painful. "*No se mueva!*"

"André, don't! He thinks you're going for a gun."

André dropped his hands and the man's hold on me eased slightly.

"Where is it?" My captor's voice was harsh but calm. Calm as if he regularly held women at knife-point. Calm as if violence was a way of life. Whatever he was looking for, when he found it, he'd kill me. Kill André. I'd never been more certain of anything.

André was frozen. Solid. Saving us was up to me.

"I don't know what you're talking about. *Yo no se.*" I put a tremor in my voice. Let my captor think I was terrified. I caught André's horrified gaze and tried to communicate with my eyes.

He was still frozen. Solid. Like a giant ice cube.

I shifted all my weight to my left leg.

"You have it." The knife pricked my skin and I felt the tickle of blood running down my neck to the collar of my new tee.

I took a quick breath, found my center, and slammed the right heel of my very sharp stiletto into the man's insole.

He gasped and loosened his grip on me.

I spun and kneed him in the groin.

He doubled over.

I clasped my hands and brought my forearms down on the back of his neck hard enough for the impact to reverberate through me.

The man fell to the ground.

I pointed to the hotel. "Run!"

André ran. Toward the villa.

Dammit. The hotel was a much better choice.

I ran after him. Slowly. Louboutins might look good and those spiky heels might make great spears for unsuspecting insoles but they made lousy running shoes.

André reached the villa long seconds before I did. He had the door open, waiting for me.

I ran inside and slammed the door.

"Call for help!" I slipped the chain in place.

André grabbed the landline and pressed the receiver to his ear. That same frozen expression returned to his face. "There's no dial tone."

"Use your cell."

I dashed past him, pulled open a kitchen drawer, and searched for a knife. The paring knife I found wouldn't do me much good against the man who'd held what felt like a machete against my throat but it was better than nothing. I put the little knife in my pocket and grabbed a heavy lamp off the end table next to the couch.

André had managed to get someone on the phone. "Send someone right away! I'm serious, Mia! We were attacked!"

He'd called Mia? Not resort security? Not the police? Mia?

I tightened my grip on the lamp and took a position next to the door, ready to swing at anyone who crossed the threshold.

The door opened—someone had a key.

The chain held.

*THUNK!*

Whoever was on the other side threw his weight against the door. The whole villa rattled.

A few more hits like that and the chain would break or the frame would splinter.

"He's here!" André screeched into the phone. "He's here!"

I gripped the heavy lamp like a baseball bat. The moment the door gave, I'd swing.

*THUNK!*

Again the villa and everything in it rattled.

"We're gonna die. We're gonna die. Mia, tell my father I—"

*Bang!*

"EEEEEEEEK!" André's *eek* was much higher and much longer than mine had been—of the shatter glass variety.

*Thump!* The sound of a body hitting the ground slipped through the crack in the door.

Then nothing.

And more nothing.

"Was that a gunshot?" André's voice shook.

I nodded.

"What do we do?"

"Wait for help." Neither the lamp nor the paring knife would do us any good against a gun.

"Poppy says it was a gunshot," André whispered into the phone. "I told you we needed help."

I flipped off the light switch next to the door and cast the villa in darkness.

"Why did you do that?" André demanded.

"Do you want someone looking through the window at us?"

"Oh. Right. Good idea."

I edged toward the glass and looked outside.

Legs splayed across the front stoop to the villa. Legs didn't worry me. Whoever shot the owner of the legs worried me. My eyes strained to see into the dark.

Nothing.

And then a crowd. Silva and Valdez, three men in hotel security uniforms, Mia, Mike, and Lord knew who else. All rushing down the path toward the villa.

The next few minutes were chaos.

Someone moved the body.

I pushed the front door closed, released the chain, and opened the door.

A tear-stained Mia brushed past the crowd of men and hugged André and me. Tightly. As if she'd never get another chance.

I hugged her back. The adrenalin that had given me strength and speed drained away.

Before the last bit of chemical energy disappeared, I

stepped outside. The man on the ground could have been with Javier at the pool—or not. It was impossible to tell. Whoever he was, death hadn't improved his looks. Especially not the black powder at his temple.

Someone had shot him at close range.

I searched my heart for feeling—horror, sadness, regret— and found emptiness. The man at my feet would have killed André and me.

"What happened?" Señor Silva was shaking—his shoulders, his hands, his head.

"He attacked us on the path but we got away. He chased us to the villa. And then..." I looked down at the body. Numb. I was still numb. "Someone shot him."

"Who? Who shot him?"

"Good question." And it was. "Here's another good question. How did he get a key card to my villa?"

"He had the key to your villa?"

"Or a master key."

Señor Silva's eyes drooped, his lips parted, and he bent at the waist.

I stepped back, sure the man was about to vomit.

Instead, he inhaled a deep breath and exhaled a string of Spanish invectives I was glad I didn't fully understand.

No one did anything. No one touched anything. Not until the police arrived.

Unfortunately, the arrival of someone in authority meant the arrival of Detective Gonzales. He scowled at me, led me into the living room, pointed at the couch, and waited for me to sit. "What happened?"

"He attacked us."

"So you say. You shot him?"

"No." I shook my head. "I don't know who shot him."

"But he's on the doorstep of your villa."

"And I was locked inside with André when he was shot."

André waved weakly from across the room.

"If you were inside and he was outside, how did he attack you?"

"He attacked us on the path. We got away and ran here."

The corners of Detective Gonzales's mouth tightened. "Miss Fields, this situation is serious."

"You don't have to tell me. Someone tried to kill me."

"Why?"

I looked toward the door where the man had died. "He wanted something."

"What?"

"I don't know." I glanced down at my hands in my lap. "He kept saying he knew she gave it to me."

"Who?"

"I assume Marta, but she didn't give me anything, and you took all her belongings with you this morning."

"Miss Fields, you must tell me the truth. This is a murder investigation. Did she give you anything?"

"No." My voice was too loud. "Nothing."

His scowl deepened and something like loathing flashed across Detective Gonzales's features.

I sat up straighter. How dare he look at me like that? None of this was my fault.

All I'd done was offer a bed to a scared woman and now people around me were dying, my friends were in danger, the police suspected me, and my brand-new $800 T-shirt was ruined.

It was official—this was the worst vacation ever.

# ELEVEN

Detective Gonzales took his time. He wanted every single detail, down to the designer of my tee-shirt (he didn't want that; but I gave it to him anyway—Rosetta Getty).

Then he turned to André, whose usually perfect hair was mussed and spikey as if he'd forgotten about his hair gel and run his fingers through the strands. "So, if I understand correctly, Miss Fields disabled the man with the knife and you ran. Anything to add, Mr. DuChamp?"

André flushed a dull red. "That about covers it." Then he sat straighter. "Given the attempt on Poppy's life, when will you return her passport?"

The detective's answering sneer told me there'd be snowmen lined up on the beach in Acapulco before I'd see my passport again.

When he ran out of questions, Detective Gonzales stood and supervised the police wheeling away the body.

I speared Silva with a look.

Like André, the manager's hair was a mess, and deep circles had formed under his eyes. He'd been looking forward to a triumphant opening. He got murders. The man looked stressed.

He should walk a mile in my Louboutins—no passport, being a suspect in a suspicious death in a foreign country, and Javier Diaz's pursuit weren't exactly soothing.

The manager regarded me with tight, tired eyes. "I guess you want another villa."

"Not tonight. But I do want the locks reprogrammed and a guard posted outside the door."

He nodded—a single, exhausted bob of his chin. "Of course."

The villa emptied until just Mia and Mike pressed against each other on the couch and André slumped in an oversize club chair. I perched on a stool at the counter.

"I don't know about you, but I could use a drink." Mia scraped the hair away from her drawn face.

Mike stood. "What can I get you?"

"Scotch. Neat."

"Two," said André.

"What about you, Poppy? Want one?" Mike crossed the room to the fully stocked bar.

"No." My nerve endings sizzled. I was too wired to drink.

Mike shrugged and poured.

André was positively haggard. He looked at me with hangdog eyes. "Poppy, I'm so sorry about tonight."

"For what?"

"I wasn't exactly heroic."

I shook my head. "Everything turned out fine."

"I should have run toward the hotel."

True. "Think about it this way—a man with a knife attacked us and we both walked away. Count it as a win."

"Still, I should have..." He glanced down at his hands. "You were like the old Poppy tonight."

"The old Poppy?"

André nodded. "The girl who rolled off the hay wagon from Bozeman."

Mia tittered.

I shot her a look. "You weren't any better with your shiny boots and sparkly buckles."

Mia preened. "I was Nashville royalty."

André smiled wistfully—as if he was seeing us as we'd been years ago. Freshman in high school overwhelmed by being new. "Nashville meant nothing at Beverly."

That was true. Too many famous people sent their kids to Beverly Hills High School; having a star parent wasn't the status symbol one would have thought.

"What I meant—" Mia gave André a look that would have killed a lesser man "—was that I wasn't a hayseed."

"And I was?" Trading barbs was infinitely better than thinking about, or talking about, the man who'd died on the other side of the front door.

"If the Louboutin fits."

My life before California had been about horses and guns and self-reliance. My father knelt in front of me when I was five years old and said, "I've seen what the world does to pretty girls. You need to be able to protect yourself." And because I'd adored him, I'd learned to fight and shoot and suppress any inclination toward pink or frills.

None of those skills had been remotely helpful at Beverly. My ability to take down the defensive tackle who made fun of Mia's accent wasn't prized. Nor was my ability to shoot a target at 100 paces. My faded Wranglers and Justin Ropers with worn heels became a source of embarrassment.

So I changed.

I told myself adapting was a new form of protecting myself.

I wasn't wrong.

Between my freshman year and graduation, the girl who'd arrived from Montana (the old Poppy) transformed into the woman I was now.

"So—" Mike handed Mia her drink then delivered one to André "—why did that guy attack you?"

"He thought Marta gave me something and he wanted it."

Mike returned to the bar and claimed his own drink. "Did she?"

"No." My voice was sharper than was strictly necessary but I'd answered that question a gazillion times.

Mike held up his free hand in surrender—as if my decking him with a heavy lamp was a possibility. "Chill."

"Give her a break, Mike," said André. "She's had a rough day."

"I was just asking."

"Man, she's dealt with three bodies and a guy with a knife at her throat."

They were talking about me as if I wasn't there—and I didn't care.

"Three?"

André held out his stretched palm. "Marta." He ticked off one finger. "Then Irene." A second finger joined the first. "Now the dude at the front door." There was the third finger.

Three lives ended. Four, if one counted Irene's husband. With that realization, the well of energy or grit or adrenaline or whatever it was keeping me going ran dry. Bone dry. I slumped on my stool. "I'm going to bed."

"It's ten o'clock." Mia, whose head never hit a pillow before two, frowned at me.

I rubbed my eyes with the heels of my palms "I'm done." Emotionally and physically and mentally and any other way there was to be done.

Mia's expression softened. "Of course you are. Do you need anything to help you sleep?"

"No. Thanks." I slid off the stool and shuffled into my bedroom, closing the door behind me.

I tossed my clothes on a chair, considered a nightgown, and decided the closet was too far away. Same with a toothbrush and the bathroom. My jewelry I put on the dresser.

Then I collapsed into bed.

The cool sheets felt heavenly and the pillows were clouds.

I closed my eyes and slept.

In my dream, I stretched into the scents of lime, basil and mandarin like a cat in a patch of sunshine. Except my sunshine was Jake's cologne.

*Click.*

The sound pulled me from my dream and my eyes flew open.

For a moment, I didn't know where I was, then everything and everyone came rushing back. I inhaled.

*Click.*

I wasn't alone.

I clutched the sheet to my chest with my left hand and made a fist with my right (those old Poppy skills would be really helpful right about now).

"Poppy."

I knew that voice—that whisper.

My right hand tightened. "You're dead."

"I'm not." He wasn't. He was alive and feet away from me, standing next to the dresser. He walked toward me, stopping at the edge of the bed.

It was him. It was Jake.

The grief that had dogged my steps burned away in an instant, consumed by rage.

The old Poppy took over.

She sat.

She swung.

She smiled when her fist connected with a jawbone.

She shimmered with pride when Jake fell to the floor.

"*Oomph.*"

The current Poppy scurried across the bed, leapt to the floor, and grabbed the discarded T-shirt.

"Ow." Jake stood, rubbing his jaw. "I guess I deserved that."

That and so much more.

"How could you?" He'd lied to me. He'd made me believe he was dead. I'd cried myself sick.

"It was for your own good." His whisper hid a world of lies.

I wanted to hit him again. Harder. Lower. Instead I reached for the phone.

"What are you doing?"

"Calling security."

"You can't."

"Watch me."

He was across the bed with his hand locked over mine in the time it took me to blink.

His touch turned the anger burning inside me incandescent.

"Let go of me." Why was I whispering? All I needed to do was scream and the security guard Silva had posted outside would be inside. André would come running. Assuming Mike was upstairs in Mia's bedroom, he'd come running too. "Let go," I whispered. A furious whisper, but a whisper nonetheless.

He released my hand. "Did Marta Vargas give you anything?"

"No." Not a whisper. But I was supremely tired of that question.

"This is important."

"No, nothing."

"Damn."

"What's going on?" I whispered. Again. Dammit. "Why are you here? How are you here?"

"I'm with an agency tasked with ending the flow of drugs from Mexico to the U.S."

"The DEA?"

"Close enough."

"You could have told me."

"I couldn't."

"Why not?"

"Too many reasons to tell."

"Why did you let me think you were dead?" I turned my head away from him. He didn't get to see my tears. "I grieved." Now my voice was barely a whisper.

"I'm sorry."

I waited for more.

And waited.

That was it? No explanation? "You're sorry?" His betrayal gutted me. I crossed my arms over my midriff and clenched my jaw.

"I am sorry. Sorrier than you'll ever know." He glanced over his shoulder at the door to the patio. "I have to go." He closed his hands around the outside of my shoulders and looked down at me, his face cast in shadows. "Please. Don't tell anyone you saw me."

He was leaving. He'd risen from the dead, snuck into my room, turned my world upside down, and he was leaving? Didn't he care what he'd put me through? Didn't he care that I'd spend the night polishing unanswered questions into shiny arrows? "You're leaving?"

"I have to." He looked down at me with troubled eyes. "Don't trust anyone."

"Like you."

Even in the darkness I could see his wince.

"I wish things could have been different." He pulled me to him and his lips closed on mine. Warm. Firm. Expert.

Like hell he could just return from the dead, breeze into my bedroom, and kiss me like he hadn't put me through the torments of the damned. He wanted different? I'd give him different.

This time I fisted with my left hand.

My knuckles connected with his jaw. Nothing could have been sweeter. "Get out."

He rubbed his jaw, the expression on his face more

surprised than pained. That was a shame. I was going for pain.

"I mean it." My voice rose. "Get out. And don't come back."

"Poppy—"

"Out!" I pointed toward the patio door. Having Jake see me cry wasn't something I wanted to contemplate.

He was halfway through the door when I said, "Wait!" My voice bumped up against the lump in my throat. "Those texts. Did you send them?"

He nodded. Once. "I wanted to keep you safe. I care about—"

"Don't." I held up my hand. I'd heard enough of his lies. And right now, my heart hurt worse than when I thought he was dead. Maybe because I'd been such a complete fool. "Just go."

---

"JAWS" played early. Billable-hours early.

"Hello." More of a mumble than an actual word.

"It's Ruth. What have you got yourself mixed up with?"

"What do you mean?"

"I've never seen such an alphabet soup of agencies. This whole Mérida Initiative is a mess."

That woke me up. "Mérida? What is that?"

"U.S., Mexican, and Central American government agencies are working together to combat drug trafficking, organized crime, and money laundering."

Oh. "Which letters of the alphabet are in the soup?"

"The usual ones. DEA. CIA. FBI. And a few I've never heard of before. But, that's not our only problem."

Of course it wasn't. "What else?"

"Do you want the bad news or the worse news?"

"Start with bad, I haven't had any coffee yet."

"Detective Gonzales is really *Agent* Gonzales. You're mixed up with a drug sting."

"The worse news?"

"There's no such person as *Jake Smith*. You were dating a ghost."

The hole in my stomach grew. Exponentially. Not even his name had been real. I was such an idiot.

"Since he's a ghost. He's probably not dead."

He definitely wasn't dead.

I swallowed. "I have my own bad news."

"Oh?"

"Someone tried to kill me last night."

"What!" Ruth's nine-hundred-dollars-an-hour voice actually cracked. "What happened?"

"A man with a knife attacked me on the path to my villa."

"Random?"

"No. I was the target. You've got to get me out of here."

"I'm trying. This multi-jurisdictional situation is a problem."

"But I haven't done anything."

"I know that, Poppy. Be patient."

Patient? Seriously? "Yesterday I woke up to a dead woman in my villa. Then I went to the hospital and held Irene Vargas's hand while she died. Last night someone held a knife to my throat then chased me back to my villa where he was shot in the head. I don't have time to be patient."

"Can you leave the resort? Go someplace else?"

"I have no passport."

"Go someplace else in Mexico."

That wasn't the worst idea ever. "James is in La Paz."

"Hold on. I'll Google La Paz." The tap of her nails on her keyboard reached me loud and clear. "Okay. La Paz is only a hundred miles from Cabo. Can you get there? The movie set is sure to have security out the wazoo."

Wazoo. That was a technical legal term.

"I don't know." Me taking off across the Baja desert didn't seem like the safest idea.

"You could charter a plane or a helicopter."

That sounded safer. Sort of.

"I'll keep working on the return of your passport. If there's anything this Gonzales wants that you can give him, do it."

"He wants something I don't have."

"Well, see if you can find it."

I didn't hold out much hope.

# TWELVE

I stumbled into the kitchen for coffee. There it was. The Keurig. Surrounded by bottled water, a variety of pods, and a golden halo. I'd never seen anything so beautiful.

Mia sat at the counter with her hands wrapped around a mug.

Zombies the morning after the apocalypse probably looked better than she did.

I tiptoed past her, afraid she might eat my brains or bite my head off (more likely). Under the best of circumstances, Mia was not a morning person. When I safely reached the Keurig, I ventured, "You're up early."

She grunted and stared at me with bleary eyes. "Mike snores. I always forget that."

Now that she mentioned it, I heard a low rumble. "That's not the air conditioner?"

"Air conditioners are much quieter."

"So you didn't sleep?"

"Not at all."

"Why didn't you just send him back to his room?"

"He doesn't believe he snores."

*Thud.*

We turned our heads toward the sound on the stairs.

André appeared at the bottom and glared at Mia. "Is there a water buffalo in your room?"

Mia shrugged. "It's Mike."

"Warn a guy." André rubbed his sunken cheeks. "I could have found a quieter room at a gun range."

Mia rolled her eyes. "Drama queen." She was just being like that because that's what Mia and André did—bickered like siblings.

"What's that?" André pointed to the emerald green minaudiere on the counter. The little bag looked especially verdant against the dove gray granite of the countertop.

"That is a handbag." Wasn't it obvious?

"Looks like a piece of kryptonite."

Mia rolled her eyes again. "It's a Baker Street."

"A what?" André scrunched up his face and rubbed his eyes. "Where are the coffee mugs?"

"Cabinet to the left of the sink," I replied. "And I second André's question, a what?"

"You don't know what it is?" Mia picked up the little bag and stroked its emerald edges with an almost reverent touch.

"Oh, please. The only reason you know about esoteric bags is because you were looking at starting that handbag line."

"I still am."

"You are? I thought you gave up on that idea."

"No. I gave up on the hair extensions idea. The handbags might happen."

André pushed the Keurig's button with unnecessary force. "Tell us about your handbag plans later. Right now—" he pointed "—tell us about that thing."

"It was handmade by artisans in Dover of all places. It retails for upwards of ten thousand."

"Dollars?" Now André ran his hand across his stubble-darkened chin. "I'm in the wrong business."

Mia smirked at him "No you're not. You make ten thousand dollars a day matching reality stars with charcoal powder for their teeth." She shifted her gaze to me. "I'm surprised you didn't tell me about this."

"About what?"

"The bag." She held it up so we could all admire its shiny greenness.

"What about it?"

"Um, when you got it? Where you got it? You usually text me pictures before a major purchase like this."

"But it's your bag." A queasiness in my stomach told me I wasn't going to like what Mia said next.

"No, it's not."

The sour feeling in my stomach was right.

We all stared at the handbag. It glowed in the morning light pouring through the kitchen window. But, unlike the Keurig with its golden halo, the green aura surrounding the bag was sinister.

"Where did it come from?" asked André.

"I grabbed it when I was helping Poppy pack," Mia explained.

I rubbed my eyes (something I seldom did because Chariss assured me the stress on my skin would give me wrinkles). "Where was it?"

"Peeking out from underneath the couch."

I swallowed. "You thought I left a ten-thousand-dollar bag on the floor?"

"You did go wading in a fountain in a pair of Jimmy Choos."

"One time!" And I'd drunk too much Moët (Champagne provided by Mia). And we'd just graduated from high school. "You're going to have to let that go."

"They were my shoes."

André held up his hands—he'd heard this argument before. "So, if it's not yours—" André nodded to Mia "—or yours—" he nodded in my direction "—who does it belong to?"

"Marta." It was the only explanation and the reason for my stomach's queasiness.

Her name hung in the air. Like a pulsing green neon sign.

"What's inside?" I was afraid of the answer.

Mia opened the little bag and pulled out a box of breath mints and a room key. "Nothing." She put the bag down on the counter and stared at it with a furrowed brow. "They're called Baker Streets because of the puzzle."

"The puzzle?" André tilted his head.

"Mmmmhm. Baker Streets for Sherlock Holmes."

"What kind of puzzle?" I asked.

She picked up the bag and turned it in her hands. "Each bag has a hidden compartment."

The bag was no bigger than two fists pressed together. What could a hidden compartment in a bag that size hold? "It's so tiny. Why bother?"

Mia rolled her eyes. "Not everyone hates party drugs, Poppy."

Oh.

André ran his hand over his stubbly chin again. "Do you think you can open it?"

Mia turned her cerulean gaze his way and raised a single brow. "Of course." Mia was one of *those* people—one who was good at things like algebra and physics and puzzles. Just don't ask her to boil water.

André and I watched as she ran her fingers over the little bag, pushing here, poking there.

"This would be easier without an audience." She sounded put out.

"Probably." I didn't move a muscle or shift my gaze.

André sipped his coffee. "It really does look like a piece of kryptonite."

"Is kryptonite a real thing?" I wondered out loud.

"No," snapped Mia. "Didn't either of you pay attention in chemistry?"

I couldn't speak for André but the only thing I remembered was that the peanut butter in the cafeteria tasted like lead. PB. Lead. The sole entry on the periodic table that stuck with me.

"Please." André rolled his eyes at Mia. "You only paid attention because you had a crush on Mr. Lewis." André made a good point. The high school chemistry teacher had been crush-worthy (not crush-worthy enough for me to pay attention in class but Mia's brain worked differently).

She twisted the handle, poked at a little bit of kryptonite, and a tiny panel opened.

"What's in there?" I leaned forward.

"A flash drive."

Oh, hell. "We should call Agent Gonzales."

"I thought he was a detective."

"Whatever." I wasn't ready to tell them about my conversation with Ruth.

"Let's plug it in," said André.

Such a bad idea. "We need to call the authorities."

"Where's your Mac?" André looked around as if I hadn't spoken.

"We need to call the authorities." It was a point worth repeating.

"It's in her room."

André hurried off, returning seconds later with my MacBook.

"What's your password?"

No way was I telling him. "This is a terrible idea."

"Her password is Conroy1."

"Conroy?" André typed with two fingers. "Is that a digit for the one or spelled out?"

"A digit and Conroy because Pat Conroy is one of her favorite authors."

I needed new friends.

My ex-friend entered the password and plugged in the flash drive. "It's a Word file."

"Really?" I looked over his shoulder and saw Spanish. "What does it say?" I couldn't read a lick but André was four-years old before his parents realized he didn't speak any English.

Rosita, the housekeeper who raised him, had spoken to him in only her native tongue.

He was still fluent.

He scanned the document. "It's an assessment of the Zetas."

"Who or what are the Zetas?" asked Mia.

"A cartel," André replied.

"That's helpful." Mia's tone dripped sarcasm. She held up her phone. "Siri, who are the Zetas?"

Siri filled her in. The Zetas were a drug cartel formed when a group of mercenaries turned on their former bosses in the Gulf Cartel. The Zetas were into drug trafficking, sex trafficking, and gun running. The original members were given numbers as names—the first leader was Z1 and so on. The cartel controlled much of southern Mexico but their base was in Nuevo Laredo across the border from Laredo, Texas.

André continued reading. "According to this, the Zetas' power structure has splintered with the arrest or death of most of the numbered Zetas. There's lots of infighting—partly due to the Mexican army's new focus on burning poppy fields in southern Mexico." André glanced at me and grinned. "Poppy fields—that's what it says. Poppy fields."

I gave him the arctic look he deserved.

"What else?" Mia read over his shoulder. Or pretended to —her Spanish wasn't any better than mine.

"This says the Zetas' disarray is an opportunity for the Sinaloans. They intend to take over Nuevo Laredo and have identified a new source of heroin."

"A new source of heroin?" Mia asked.

"They need one because of the burnt poppy fields." André glanced my way then quickly returned his gaze to the screen. "Okay, it's an old source of heroin that's new to Mexico."

"What do you mean?" Again Mia tried reading over André's shoulder. She caught her lip between her teeth. She squinted. Nothing helped. She still couldn't read Spanish. "Siri, which country produces the most heroin?"

Siri's answer was Afghanistan.

"The Sinaloans are going into business with someone named Ahmed Badawi." André pointed to an incomprehensible portion of the document.

"Who?"

"Siri—"

"Give Siri a rest, Mia. I'll Google it." André's fingers flew over the keys.

Google gave us a quick answer. In English. Ahmed Badawi was an Afghani heroin dealer and terrorist wanted by the Département de la Sûreté for a bombing in a Paris café that killed twelve and by MI5 for a bombing in the London tube that killed twenty-seven.

I dropped my face to my hands and wished with all my heart that I'd never stepped foot in James' Gulfstream. We were in so much trouble. "So, if I understand this correctly—" I peeked through my fingers at my gob-smacked friends "—the Sinaloans are going to war with the Zetas and into business with the largest heroin producer in the world who also happens to be a terrorist."

"Looks that way." André wore a stunned expression.

I needed more coffee. I stood and pointed at the drive. "We have to give that to Gonzales."

"Fine," said Mia. "But we're not giving him the bag."

"Why not?"

"This bag is a work of art. Gonzales can have the flash

drive. Put it an ordinary bag and say it belonged to Marta. I'm keeping this one."

I opened my mouth to argue but Mia wore her stubborn face. I'd have better luck arguing with a mule. Plus, there were more important things at stake than the final disposition of Marta's handbag.

"Fine," I ceded. "Go pack."

"Pack?" Her brows rose.

I nodded. "Both of you."

"Why?" André turned away from the computer screen and scowled at me. "We're not going anywhere."

"Yes, you are. Gonzales already has my passport. Do you want him to take yours too?"

André crossed his arms. "We're not leaving you here."

"It's a five-star resort. I'll be fine."

"You were attacked. Just last night." He made a good point.

I waved it away. "After I hand this drive over to Gonzales, no one will have the slightest interest in me. Gonzales might even return my passport." There was a better chance of pigs flying over Tijuana—especially if Gonzales figured out I'd looked at the drive.

My friends remained stony-faced, unimpressed, and unmoved by my persuasive skills.

"Please." I pressed my hands together as if in prayer. "Go. I need you two to be safe. Go to the airport. Charter a plane. Please. I won't call Gonzales until I know you're safely in the United States."

"We can't possibly leave you." Mia shook her head.

"There's no point in all of us getting stuck here." I pushed the Keurig's buttons and watched it spit coffee into my cup. "If you're that worried, I can stay with James in La Paz."

My best friend regarded me through narrowed eyes. "You mean that?"

I crossed my heart. "I do. I'll call him at nine o'clock."

André's brows drew together. "Is it suddenly quiet in here?"

It was. The ailing-air-conditioner snoring was gone.

How long had it been quiet? Jake's warning flashed through my head. *Trust no one.*

André pulled the drive out of my Mac and closed the lid. Quickly.

A second later Mike traipsed down the stairs. "What's a guy got to do to get a cup of coffee?"

The question wasn't if he'd been listening. He had been. I knew it in my gut. The question was for how long?

# THIRTEEN

When I knew Mia and André were in the air, I made the call.
"Señor Silva, this is Poppy Fields calling."

"Si, Señorita." His voice was that of a man waiting for the
next shoe to drop.

"I—we—found something we believe belonged to Marta
Vargas. Would you please make arrangements for me to meet
Detective Gonzales in your office at one o'clock?"

"In my office?" Anyplace-but-here was evident in his
voice along with a *soupçon* of why-me, and a dash of this-
*gringa*-is-ruining-my-life.

"Your office." Things would go better if Gonzales didn't
know Mia and André had run back to the United States at my
behest. "I'm sure you understand when I tell you I'm tired of
having police in and out of where I'm staying."

He sighed. "You are right, Señorita. One o'clock?"

"Or two." I could be magnanimous.

"And you found something that belonged to Marta
Vargas? What is it?"

*Trust no one.*

"I'll let Detective Gonzales tell you about it." I'd put the flash drive (along with the breath mints and the room key) in a plain black clutch. "Ask him to bring my passport."

"I'll ask." He didn't sound hopeful.

You'd think the man would move heaven and earth to get my passport returned. Getting me and the chaos surrounding me out of his resort had to be a priority.

"*Gracias.*" I hung up the phone and called James.

"Poppy!" Unlike Señor Silva, James' voice was warm. "How are you?"

"I have a problem—problems." I gave him the condensed version of everything that had happened since I last saw him (minus Jake in my bedroom). "Would you please send the plane? If I get my passport back, I'll head to Los Angeles. If I don't, I'd like to come to you. Ruth Gardner thinks I'd be safer in La Paz."

"I'll send the plane right away. It will be waiting for you whenever you get to the airport. What else can I do? Are there strings we can pull?"

"If there are strings to be pulled, Ruth is already pulling them. If you'll just send the plane."

"Consider it done."

"Thank you, James." Tears welled in my eyes.

"Honey, I love you like you're my own daughter. We're going to make sure you're safe and we're going to get you out of this mess."

"I love you too, James. Thank you."

At a quarter till one, I walked up the jasmine-scented path to the main hotel and asked for Señor Silva. A pretty woman with a gentle smile led me to his office. She tapped softly on the door.

"Come in." The hotel manager's voice still rasped.

I took a deep breath and stepped inside.

Detective Gonzales sat across a huge desk from Señor Silva. Calling him Detective was important. He'd lied to me about who he worked for. For a reason. Calling him Agent Gonzales might antagonize him.

I took the other chair in front of the desk, settled my tote next to the chair's legs, then crossed my ankles and folded my hands in my lap.

"You have something to give me?" demanded Detective Gonzales.

"I do." With an apologetic smile, I explained how Mia and I had confused the bag's ownership. Then I pulled the little black clutch out of my tote.

Detective Gonzales practically snatched the small purse from my hands.

He opened the flap and spotted the flash drive. His eyes glowed with an emotion I didn't care to name. "Your friends will corroborate your story?"

"Of course." They were safely in the U.S—out of his reach.

His eyes narrowed. "Did you look at the drive?"

"No." A justifiable lie. "May I have my passport back? Please?"

"I will review what's on the drive."

"What difference does the drive's contents make to returning my passport?" I drew myself up straight (tough to do in the leather club chair). "I did as you asked. I brought the drive to you as soon as I found it."

"I want to make sure it's legitimate before returning anything."

It never occurred to me to give Detective Gonzales a fake flash drive. My mouth gaped open. "But—"

"It won't take long. A day or two at most."

First off, a day or two seemed like an eternity. Second, I didn't believe him. "I don't carry around spare flash drives when I go on vacation." Did he think I just genied one out of thin air? "Where would I get one?"

"We sell them in the gift shop." Señor Silva leaned

forward and peered at the tiny item in Detective Gonzales's hand. "That brand."

"Plug it in now." I pointed at Señor Silva's terminal. Señor Silva suddenly looked as if he'd eaten a plate of bad shrimp.

Gonzales shook his head. "There could be sensitive information."

"Or it could be Irene Vargas's recipe for chicken mole."

That earned me one of Gonzales' sneers.

"Detective, since I've been here, I've found a body, held a woman's hand while she died, and been attacked by a man who was later murdered on my doorstep. I want my passport and I want to go home."

Silva nodded with enthusiasm. Me with a passport was me out of his resort (he should have thought about that before he opened his trap about the flash drives in the gift shop).

Gonzales didn't react to my plea. "A few days at most—"

A few days? I stood. "It appears we have nothing more to discuss. You'll be hearing from my lawyer." I strode out of the office with my back straight and my head held high.

I strode right into the light, airy lobby and stopped a few feet in front of the concierge's desk. That desk. Not as big as Señor Silva's but three times nicer. It had patina. It belonged in a patrón's office on a hacienda.

The woman behind the desk spoke into the phone. Rapid Spanish. I couldn't understand a word.

The tanned, blonde, glamorous, probably-shilled-on-Instagram-for-a-living couple seated at her desk looked on expectantly.

I looked at the ceiling and fingered the locket at my neck. The poor woman didn't need three people watching her talk.

"Gracias." She hung up the phone and smiled at the couple.

"You got the table?" asked the Ken-doll man.

"Yes."

"The one we wanted? The VIP section with the best view of the stage?"

"Yes, sir."

"I just want to make sure because I—"

I sighed.

Barbie looked over her shoulder, saw me, and poked Ken in the ribs.

Ken turned and looked at me. "Hey, aren't you Chariss—"

"I'm her daughter."

"You're Poppy Fields," said Barbie. "I follow you on Twitter. I'm so excited to meet you." She dug in her pool bag, pulled out a book, and held it up. "I always read your recommendations."

Oh. Wow. "I loved that one."

"Me, too. I can't wait to see how it ends but I also want it to go on forever. Do you ever feel that way about a book?"

"All the time." I'd wronged this woman. Her name wasn't Barbie.

Ken stood and pulled on not-Barbie's elbow. "We're due for our couple's massage."

Not-Barbie stood. "It was a pleasure meeting you. I'm Barbara—" she glanced at her left hand where an enormous diamond ring sparkled "—Barbara Brown. This is my husband, Ken."

Seriously? "It was nice meeting you, too."

"Do you think we could grab a picture?" Already Barbie-not-Barbie was handing her phone to the concierge.

We smiled for the camera then Barbie-not-Barbie and Ken headed off to their massage without leaving the woman who'd secured their table a tip.

"May I help you?" The concierge sounded tired—as if sitting behind a desk (even a nice desk), fielding unreasonable demands from guests who didn't tip wasn't her dream job.

"I need a car to the airport, please."

"At what time?"

"Immediately. The plane is waiting."

The concierge tapped a few keys. "We have a shuttle leaving in thirty minutes."

"I'd prefer a car."

She drew her brows together and tapped at more keys. "An hour. I can get you a car in an hour."

"Perfect." I gave her my villa number and deposited a thousand peso note on the desk. "Thank you."

Her gaze swept over the bill. "We hope you'll come again soon."

Not in a million years. I rose from the chair, turned, and bumped into Brett.

"Poppy!" His hands closed briefly on my shoulders.

"I'm sorry Brett. I didn't see you standing there. Are you waiting for the concierge?"

"No. I saw you from across the lobby."

Oh goody. How much had he heard? I reviewed my conversation with the helpful woman behind the desk. All I'd done was request a car.

"You're leaving the resort?"

He'd heard me.

"I am."

"Where are you off to?"

None of his business. "I'm off to finish packing. The concierge has arranged for a car for me." I stepped away from him.

He stopped me with an uninvited hand on my arm. "I meant, where are you going?"

None of his damn business. "I'm due in Paris at the end of the week."

The corner of his mouth ticked as if I'd annoyed him.

"I need to go." I tugged against his grasp.

Brett held tight. "Where are you going?"

"There you are!" Mike draped an arm around my shoulders. "I've been looking for you. You promised me a drink."

I pulled free of Brett's grasp on my arm and smiled up at Mike, who smelled like beer and sunscreen. An unlikely combination for a hero.

Brett's face turned the color of old bricks and the tic at the corner of his mouth did the merengue.

"Mike, do you know Brett Cannon? Brett, this is my friend Mike Wilde."

They eyed each other. Nodded with tight jerks of their chins. There was a story there.

"Mike, will you walk me back to the villa? We can have that drink while I pack."

"Of course." Mike smiled as if walking me to the villa was the absolute best offer he'd ever had.

"Nice seeing you again," I said to Brett. "Goodbye."

Brett smoothed the annoyance off his features. At least, he tried—there was nothing he could do about that tic. "Nice seeing you, too."

Mike and I stepped outside onto the sun-drenched veranda. "You looked like you needed saving." He shook his blond head. "Plus, that guy's bad news."

I tilted my head and looked up at him. "How do you know Brett?"

Mike's expression turned grim. "Long story. Believe me when I tell you, he's bad news."

"Well, thanks for being my white knight."

"Can I buy you a drink?"

I shook my head. "I need to pack."

"Where are you going?"

"I'm going to La Paz to see James."

"Ballester? Why?"

If I told Mike the whole story—my dead ex-boyfriend showed up in the middle of the night insisting I was in danger, I'd already sent Mia and André back to Los Angeles, I was stuck in Mexico, and I was scared—I wouldn't have time to pack. I didn't have time to recount even half that story. Plus —*trust no one*. "He needs me for a bit part in his movie."

"Don't!"

Heads turned.

I pulled on his arm. "Let's walk."

"I mean it, Poppy. Don't. Do anything but what Chariss does. Believe me—" the bitterness in his voice could curdle milk "—the comparisons will never end."

"Maybe you're right." It wasn't as if I had any interest in being in a movie. "I might just hang out with James."

His face cleared. Slightly.

"Trust me on this one."

I did. We walked the rest of the way to the villa in silence.

At the door, I rose up on my tiptoes and kissed Mike's cheek. "Thanks again for saving me."

"Is Mia here?"

"She and André took off for parts unknown." Almost true.

Mike sighed as if he wished he'd gone with them. "Well, have Mia call me."

"Will do."

When I got inside, I called Gardner, Wilson and Bray. "Ruth Gardner, please."

"Ms. Gardner is in a meeting. May I take a message?"

Of course she was in a meeting. Ruth was always in a meeting. "Would you please tell her Poppy Fields called. James Ballester is sending his plane. I'll be leaving Cabo in an hour."

"Anything else, Ms. Fields?"

"Tell her I still don't have a passport."

"Yes, ma'am."

I hung up the phone and packed. Candles, a cashmere throw, framed pictures in one suitcase. Shoes and handbags, all carefully wrapped in chamois bags, in another. A dedicated case for make-up, lotions, and potions. Two large bags for my clothes. Then my laptop, a clean pair of underwear, and a small notebook in my messenger bag.

I finished just as a black Escalade parked outside.

I opened the front door.

"Señorita Fields," said a man in a polo shirt embroidered with the resort's logo, "I am Juan. I will take you to the airport."

"Thank you."

I climbed into the back seat with my messenger bag. Juan loaded the suitcases into the back. Together, we were on our way.

"Did you enjoy your stay?" he asked.

Not at all. "It's a beautiful property."

Juan and his Escalade whisked me through crowded streets then entered the near empty toll road.

*Ding.*

I glanced at my phone.

*You okay?*

I texted Mia back. *On my way to the airport. Still no passport. Call Mike. I didn't tell him you left…*

The phone rang. Sure it was Mia, I answered without looking at the number. "Hey."

"Polly? Barclift O'Neill calling." My agent. My heart fluttered.

"Sorry, Barclift. I thought you were someone else. How are you?"

"There's been interest in your book."

"Oh?" I didn't dare hope. I crossed the fingers of my left hand.

"There's a pre-emptive bid."

"A what?"

"One of the publishers likes it so much they've offered a hefty advance to acquire it without my going to the other publishers for counter-offers."

"How hefty?"

In front of me the driver fixed his gaze in the rearview and muttered softly.

I looked over my shoulder. A Range Rover followed us too closely.

"Seven figures."

Wow. Seven-figures had my full attention. I sat in stunned silence.

"Are you there?" Barclift sounded amused.

Someone had spilled the beans. There was no way Polly Feld's book would sell for that much. Numbers like those just didn't happen. "Did you tell them who I am?"

Now Barclift was silent for a moment. "Who are you?"

I'd told Barclift my name was Polly Feld. What should I tell him now?

"*Pinche estúpido!*"

Impact jarred through me and the seatbelt cut across my chest.

Plus, there was that awful sound of metal scraping, bending, collapsing.

I blinked, disoriented.

What had we hit?

A twisted, rattletrap Jeep wrapped around the Escalade's front fender.

The road was deserted. How had Juan hit that?

I glanced out the side window. There were men. Running. In masks. With guns.

I spoke so fast my tongue tripped. "Barclift, my real name is Poppy Fields and I think I'm being kidnapped. Call Ruth Gardner at Gardner, Wilson & Bray. She'll—" the Escalade's door flew open and an enormous man in a black ski mask grabbed my phone.

Then he grabbed me.

# FOURTEEN

The man who snatched my phone (and me) dropped the phone on the ground and crushed the casing beneath the heel of his boot with one glass-shattering stomp. If that was to be my fate, I wasn't going quietly. I swung at him. I curled my fingers into claws and scratched at him. I kicked.

I was a kitten fighting a Grizzly bear.

"*No la lastimes,*" barked a man holding what looked like a gold-plated AK-47.

I stopped struggling and gaped at his gun. Were those pave diamonds glinting on the hand guard? Were the diamonds in the shape of a skull?

The Grizzly bear dragged me away from my crumpled phone and the crumpled Escalade.

The barking man scanned the sky.

A smaller man who reeked of testosterone and gun oil took over for the Grizzly. In a fair fight, I might have bested him. But he jabbed the muzzle of a Glock into my ribs. I couldn't fight a gun.

This couldn't be happening. Could not.

Except there was the Escalade with the driver slumped over the wheel. Was he injured? Was he dead? Was he faking?

The man with the gun in my ribs picked up a strand of my hair, sniffed it, and said something I didn't need to understand to understand. His intentions transcended language.

"Get away from me!"

The barking man lowered his gaze from the sky and fixed his dark eyes on the man rubbing my hair between the pads of his fingers. A string of invectives followed and the man with the Glock in my ribs released my hair as if his fingers had been seriously burned.

I was in so much trouble. "What do you want?"

They didn't answer me. They didn't move. They stared at the sky—waiting. For what?

A speck appeared in the unrelenting blue. A speck that grew bigger and louder with each passing second.

Then it landed on the ground. On the toll road. As if the pilot made stops at kidnappings all the time.

The helicopter was enormous. White with a deep blue belly and rotors that went on for miles.

The man with the gun pushed me toward the chopper.

Getting in that chopper was a terrible idea. At least here, I knew where I was. Maybe I could get to the Escalade, shove Juan out of the driver's seat, and escape. The liquids dripping from the engine made that seem unlikely. Or, I could run. But where? There was nothing around me but desert and masked men with guns.

The man with the Glock pushed me again. Hard. A man who'd been denied something he wanted, he was now taking whatever opportunity he could to wrest his revenge. *"Muevete."*

Climbing aboard that helicopter seemed like the worst idea I'd had all week—and it had been a week chock-full of bad ideas.

If I stalled long enough, would help come? Maybe Barclift had believed me and called for help. Maybe there was a panic button in the Escalade, and maybe Juan had pushed it. Maybe I was delusional.

"*Muevete.*" The man with the Glock pushed me again.

I fell. On purpose. My wrist twisted when I landed and a rock dug into my knee. "Ouch!"

*Bang!*

The man with the Glock fell too. Next to me. A small hole darkened the skin between his eyes.

My heart beat so fast I worried it might explode. Had that bullet been meant for me?

The Grizzly bear extended his hand to me, ignoring the corpse that had been a living, breathing person only seconds ago. "*Está bien*?"

I swallowed, took Grizzly's hand (I didn't have much choice), and stared at the place our flesh touched. The back of Grizzly's hand was tattooed with a vicious claw.

He helped me off the asphalt—gently—his forehead wrinkled with concern. "*Está bien*?" he repeated.

No. I wasn't *bien*. I shook my head and stumbled away from the body as my stomach rejected everything in it.

I bent over and threw up for a solid hour (maybe not quite an hour).

When I finally stood straight, Grizzly pressed a clean handkerchief into my hand.

I wiped my mouth.

"*Hay agua en el helicóptero.*"

My options were few (none). I nodded and stumbled toward the helicopter and, if I understood Grizzly correctly, water.

What I didn't know about helicopters could fill a book. But even in my ignorance, I could tell this one cost a fortune.

The interior was finished in cream leather with seats so inviting they looked as if they belonged in Chariss's private screening room.

Grizzly helped me climb inside.

"Very safe helicopter," said the barker. He offered me a smile and a nod and pointed to one of the cushy seats with the muzzle of his gun. "Buckle." Then he shut the door on me.

I pressed my face to the glass. There was the destroyed Jeep and the destroyed Escalade and the dead man on the ground.

I tried the handle but it didn't move.

Dammit.

I collapsed into one of the leather chairs and watched Grizzly and Barker climb into their Range Rover and drive away as if killing a man and abducting a woman was just another day at the office.

On the console next to my seat sat an ice bucket filled with chilled water bottles. There were flowers. There was a television.

The increased whir of the rotors spinning was quickly followed by the helicopter leaving the ground.

I buckled (difficult the way my hands shook) and looked out the window.

We flew away from the afternoon sun, crossing the aqua-marine Sea of Cortez.

What was across the sea from Baja?

I pictured a map of Mexico.

Sinaloa. The helicopter was crossing the water to Sinaloa. The map in my mind was replaced by the memory of handing over the drive with the Sinaloa Cartel's plans for Nuevo Laredo and the heroin trade to Agent Gonzales.

I gave up looking out the window, dropped my head to my hands, and took stock.

I had no phone, no computer, no weapon, and no way of knowing where I was going.

No one was coming to save me.

On the positive side of the equation—I groaned. There was no positive side. I'd been kidnapped by a drug cartel.

Land appeared.

Below me was a city. A city as distant and removed as a star. Probably as cold too. If I somehow got free, I didn't imagine I'd find warm welcomes in the towns of Sinaloa.

Then came mountains. Lots of them. Rugged terrain.

I opened a bottle of water and made myself drink it.

I fought tears.

I cradled my aching wrist in my lap.

The pilot circled a landing pad and dropped out of the sky.

The landing skids touched down.

The rotors slowed.

And the fear that had been nibbling at me took an enormous bite.

Why had the cartel gone to all this trouble? If they wanted me dead, they could have killed me on the road from the resort. What did they want me from me?

The door to the helicopter opened and Javier Diaz smiled at me. "Welcome."

My body froze. Ice cubes had more mobility.

That's the only reason I didn't scurry into a corner of the helicopter when he reached for my hand.

"I'm so glad you're safe. I told Ignacio you were coming to visit and he has cut his trip short. He'll be here in two days." He held up two fingers and his smile broadened.

My vocal chords were frozen too.

Javier took my hand but he didn't pull me out of the chopper. Instead he spoke slowly, gently, as if he were calming a spooked horse. "You were in terrible danger. You're safe here."

Here appeared to be a mountain top. I glanced past Javier. An enormous lemon-yellow hacienda looked down on the valleys below.

"That's Ignacio's house," Javier crooned.

"Who's Ignacio?" My voice, barely thawed, was hardly a whisper.

"Ignacio Quintero."

The face of illegal drugs in Mexico. Pictures of him graced the evening news at least once a week.

My voice froze again.

"Shall we go inside? I've asked the chef to prepare a meal for us but it won't be ready for another hour or so." He squeezed my hand. "I can give you a tour. The house is spectacular."

I'd expect nothing less from the biggest drug lord in the world.

I didn't move.

Javier regarded me carefully. He took in the rip in the knee of my pants and the way I held my injured wrist against my body. "Are you hurt?" Javier's voice acquired a sharp edge. "I told those *estúpidos* you were precious. I told them to treat you better than they treat their mothers. Nothing was to happen to you."

Those *estúpidos* had killed a man standing next to me. True, the man had held a gun to my ribs and harbored unspeakable intentions but I'd tripped on purpose. That made his death my fault. Those *estúpidos* had also bundled me on to a helicopter without a word as to my destination. No matter how many fresh hankies Grizzly offered, the eyes of those *estúpidos* had been filled with death.

Exactly like Javier's.

I shuddered.

"Come inside." Javier pulled softly on my uninjured hand. "Please. We have a medic. And—" his gaze took in my light linen tunic and pants, with his free arm he waved at the surrounding mountains "—it gets chilly up here when the sun goes down. Let's get you inside."

I didn't have much (any) choice.

I climbed down from the helicopter and got a better look

at my surroundings. We were on the tallest mountain in the range. There was an enormous house and a tennis court and gardens and fountains and men with automatic rifles.

I shivered.

"You're cold. Let's get you inside. A coffee? A brandy? What will warm you up?" Javier was acting like an attentive host not a kidnapper.

"A ride back to Cabo."

"It's too dangerous."

"Los Angeles?"

"Ignacio would never forgive me if he didn't get a chance to meet you. This way." He rested one hand on the small of my back and gently pushed me toward the house.

I allowed myself to be pushed.

We reached the front door and Javier opened it with a flourish.

Inside, a man with a ponderous mustache and an equally ponderous belly raced by. His cowboy boots slipped on the tile floor and he fell, whacking his knee.

"What are you doing?" Javier demanded.

"*Consuela se escapo.*"

Javier paled.

A second man, this one with a plaid shirt straining across his belly, ran through the foyer, the heels of his boots pounding against the tiles. His hair was wild. His eyes were wilder.

Who or what was Consuela that she could cause so much consternation? Were they running after her or from her?

Javier manufactured a weak smile. "Ignacio keeps an amazing stable. Do you like horses? I'll show them to you while they deal with Consuela."

A third *sicario,* this one without a mustache (he made up for it with extra belly), dashed through the foyer and followed his comrades into the room to our right.

No way was I missing catching a glimpse of Consuela

who could make Javier pale and grown men—killers, *sicarios* —dash around like scared children

"*Consuela, tengo un regalo para ti.*" The *sicario* version of baby-talk was a frightening thing. Especially when coming from a man made up of hard fat and dead eyes.

I stepped all the way into the house and looked to the right.

Consuela had disappeared into an enormous room filled with overstuffed couches, Spanish Colonial antiques, and a fireplace that could serve as a parking spot for a Mini-Cooper. Above the fireplace hung a portrait of my mother.

The artist had painted Chariss in a red off-the-shoulder gown. She wore a mantilla. Her expression was soft, and sweet, and kind. She stared lovingly out at the room.

Art had totally strayed from reality.

There was a flurry of movement in the corner where No-Mustache bent from the waist and held out his hand. "*Toma.*"

"*Ay!*" He jumped up and down and clutched his hand. His jaw worked. "*Quiero matar a esa perra.*"

I didn't understand what he'd said, but I understood the tone. Things were looking bleak for Consuela.

Something spun past him. A dervish? A Tasmanian devil?

Javier stepped in front of me. "Really, you should see the stables. Ignacio breeds Aztecas. They are a cross between Andalusians and Quarter Horses. They are the national horse of Mexico. Very beautiful." He took my arm and steered me toward the door.

I dug in my heels. "What is Consuela?"

"Just a dog." His insouciant shrug was at odds with the chaos in the living room.

Plaid-Shirt lunged, missed, and fell into a side table. The exhaustive list of curses that escaped his lips suggested his hip had caught the table's corner.

"*Cállate, la estás asustando,*" shouted the first *sicario*—the one with a mustache and a belly and a voice that could chill blood.

"What did he say?"

"He's concerned the shouting is scaring Consuela."

The men were the ones who looked scared.

The first *sicario* took charge. He pointed No-Mustache to one end of a massive couch and Plaid-Shirt to the other end. They had the dog cornered.

The first *sicario* leaned over the couch's back as if he meant to snatch the dog from above.

The couch had other ideas. Unaccustomed to an oversized man leaning over its over-stuffed back, it tilted. For an instant, it balanced on two legs. Then it fell. With the man.

The crash shook the house.

"Consuela!" No-Mustache and Plaid-Shirt had no interest in the first *sicario's* welfare. Horror filled their voices. "Consuela!"

Consuela darted out from underneath the couch, used its twin as a springboard, and landed on a table whose centuries-old patina had heretofore not included claw marks.

*Click, click, click.*

Consuela paused at the opposite edge of the table, looked back at the fallen couch where No-Mustache and Plaid-Shirt were now attempting to extricate the third man, and (I swear this) snickered.

Then she spotted me.

She drew back her little lips, bared her little teeth, and snarled.

"We should go," said Javier. "Now."

"She's a Chihuahua."

"She's a killer."

I stared up at him. "Consuela the killer Chihuahua?"

"*Sí.*"

Consuela launched herself off the table and sprinted toward us.

Javier jumped in front of me, which might have seemed heroic if Consuela was a lion or a tiger or a puma.

The little dog jumped higher than any reasonable person would believe. Her little mouth was open. Her little eyes were filled with evil intent.

If she'd had a trampoline to give her a bit more height, she'd have ripped out Javier's throat. As it was, she ripped the breast pocket off his sport coat.

He caught her and held her far from his body.

She snarled and wriggled and snapped.

"This is Consuela." He held her out so I could get a close look.

A little dog the color of warm sand glared at me, her gaze promising a bloody death.

"She is Ignacio's pride and joy." With obvious relief, he handed her off to Plaid-Shirt. "She doesn't like strangers. Or women."

And I was both.

# FIFTEEN

With Consuela the killer Chihuahua captured and handed off to Plaid-Shirt, Javier's plans to show me the stables fell by the wayside. "I will take you to your suite."

"Listen, I appreciate you thought I was in danger but—"

"I didn't think." He wagged a finger at me and his lips curved into a smile that didn't reach his eyes. "I knew. A Zeta tried to kill you."

"Why are you so worried about my safety?"

"Ignacio wants to meet you. If anything happened to you, he'd have my head."

I suspected he meant that literally.

Javier led me down an endless hallway and flung open the door to a bedroom fit for a queen. The ceilings rose twelve feet. I'd need a stepstool to climb onto the white damask covered bed. The view out the French doors was of the sun setting behind a neighboring mountain.

"These will be your rooms."

At least if I was on the bed, I'd be out of Consuela's reach.

He glanced at his watch. "Dinner will be ready soon. I'll send the medic to look at your wrist."

"Señor Diaz—"

"Javier," he corrected. "Please, call me Javier."

If that's how he wanted it. "Javier, what's the plan? You can't keep me here forever."

"We'll talk about it at dinner."

Not encouraging.

Javier smiled and backed out of the room.

The snick of a lock told me I wouldn't be exiting until he was ready.

I hurried over to the glass doors.

Locked. Of course.

No key. Of course.

And the glass looked impossibly thick. Bulletproof. Of course.

I walked into the bathroom and found a full counter. Box after box. Chanel blush, still new in its box. I picked up the package and looked at the color. Mine. The same was true with everything from the lipsticks to the mascara. Javier had provided the right cleanser, the right serum, the right moisturizer.

Even the right brand of toothpaste.

They'd been in my villa at the resort. Gone through my things.

Creepy-crawlies skittered down my spine.

I returned to the bedroom and pulled open a dresser drawer.

Lavender sachets scented La Perla lingerie and a shell pink pajama set.

I picked up a bra. The right size.

Ugh.

Killers had gone through my underwear looking for sizes.

The shudder that racked my body shook my teeth.

*Tap, tap.*

I dropped the bra, slammed the drawer, and glanced at the locked door. "Come in."

The door swung open and a slender young man with a

first-aid kit appeared in the doorway. "My name is Manuel. Señor Diaz sent me to look at your wrist."

My wrist was sprained. And the sprain was mild. "I'm fine."

He donned an I-know-you're-probably-right-but-I-have-to-make-sure-or-someone-may-shoot-me expression. "I need to look."

These people were killers and I was alone. There was no point in antagonizing them. Not until I had a plan. "Fine."

He left the door open behind him.

For an instant, we both looked at the hallway.

"There is no place to run." Manuel's tone was apologetic. So was his shrug. "Even if you could get out of the house, the terrain is rough, and the nearest town is miles away. Even if you made it there, the people who live there are loyal to Ignacio. They would send you back."

It was as if he'd read my mind.

I held out my wrist.

He poked and prodded and squeezed. "It's a sprain."

"I know." All those classes my dad enrolled me in had meant lots of sprains. I recognized them easily.

He took an Ace bandage out of his kit and wrapped it around my wrist.

"Ice would be better," I told him.

"I will have some sent to your room but you can't wear ice to dinner."

But I could wear the bandage. And a wrapped wrist would give Javier the idea that something positive had been done.

"Will you wear it? Just for tonight?" Fear flickered in his eyes. "Please?"

"Fine."

"Thank you. I'll make sure you have the ice before you go to bed." He closed up his kit. "Señor Diaz asked me to tell you there are clean clothes in the closet."

All with the correct sizes and labels, I had no doubt.

Just how long had Javier Diaz been planning my abduction?

With a nod of goodbye, Manuel left my room, closing the door behind him.

I headed to the closet where a couple of evening gowns hung next to a La Perla nightgown with matching robe. The shoes, still in their boxes, were Jimmy Choos and Louboutins (the correct size, of course). A shelf held a Prada city saddlebag and what looked like a large purple amethyst. I stared at that amethyst—a Baker Street bag. A bag that told me they'd been through my things after Marta died.

Several kid leather boxes embossed with my favorite designers' logos were stacked on the fainting couch in the center of the little room.

Javier had thought of everything.

I sat on the fainting couch and opened a Penny Preville box.

The earrings inside sparkled up at me.

I was in a world of trouble.

Sure, right now the world was Stella McCartney gowns and—I opened a second box—Ippolita bracelets, but the path behind Javier was strewn with bodies. Somehow, I had to find a way out of Ignacio Quintero's mountain hideaway before they discovered I'd handed over the drive to Agent Gonzales.

---

DINNER WAS SERVED in the formal dining room at a table long enough for twenty.

Javier, looking like a Latin Lothario in an Armani suit, sat to the right of the empty seat at the head of the table. I sat to the left.

Candlelight from an enormous chandelier cast a rosy glow on us.

"We weren't entirely sure you'd arrive today. Tonight we are having typical Sinaloan fare. That—" he pointed at a butterflied chicken with his fork "—is *Pollo a las Brasas con Cebollitas*. Tomorrow we'll have something more elegant."

I said nothing.

"I've chosen a Vouvray to accompany our meal," Javier continued. "I hope you like it."

A stranger with an impressive mustache appeared at my shoulder and filled my glass.

Bowls of rice, guacamole, roasted potatoes, beans, and slaw filled the space between Javier and me. And silence. Javier and I had nothing to say to each other.

"You look lovely tonight." There was no warmth, no approval in Javier's eyes.

"Thank you." I'd chosen a Gucci gown and loaded my uninjured wrist with Ippolita bracelets.

More silence. Nothing but the sound of silverware against the china and the tinkle of my bracelets.

This dinner didn't feel like a meal for a kidnapper and his hostage. It felt like an incredibly awkward date—the kind where the save-me text couldn't come soon enough.

My phone was crushed on a Baja highway. No save-me text was coming. If I wanted saving, I'd have to do it myself.

"That's an unusual necklace."

My locket was an antique pave heart. My hand rose to my throat. "My father gave it to me. I never take it off."

"Tell me about him."

Tell a drug lord about my dad? I fluttered my eyelashes and borrowed the smile Chariss used to snow men. "There's not much to tell. My father died when I was in my teens." I upped the wattage on the smile. "I'd rather talk about you. How did you end up here?" I swept my hand over my plate, indicating the dining room, the house, the job.

"I was educated in the States. Then went on to get my MBA."

I raised my brows.

"This is a business. A business like any other." Javier actually sounded defensive.

"Your employees carry guns."

He shrugged. "It's a dangerous business. There's always an upstart organization who wants to take something from us —to steal part of our business. This cannot be allowed."

Like the Sinaloa Cartel wanted to take Nuevo Laredo from the Zetas.

I kept that thought to myself. "Your business—it's illegal. It hurts people."

"Americans, you're good at blaming Mexicans for the United States' drug problem. We did not create the demand. We are simply filling it."

"Didn't Pablo Escobar create a demand for cocaine?" It's amazing what could be learned binging *Narcos* on Netflix.

Javier pursed his lips. "I suppose. But one could also say that American drug companies with their opioids created a demand for heroin." He rested his elbow on the table and a smile flitted across his mouth. "I'm sure that was an unintended consequence."

"So you're comparing what you do to a pharmaceutical company?" I could hear the outrage in my voice. I needed to shut the hell up, to delve deep and locate an iota of Chariss's charm. Because, in a similar situation, Chariss would be charming. Chariss would not poke the bear. Chariss would have the bear eating out of her hand.

"In many ways, we are like a pharmaceutical company. But our drugs don't require a prescription."

I bit my tongue.

"Yours is a country of children looking for easy fixes. Take a pill. Snort a line. Cover the pain rather than dealing with it."

"Not everyone is like that."

"Give it another generation."

Be charming. Be charming. "May we agree to disagree?"

He nodded and the silence returned.

I ate a bite of chicken. "This is delicious."

He grunted.

Be charming. "How did you meet Marta?"

For half a second something alive and grief-stricken shone in his eyes. "I financed one of her movies. She was special."

So special he'd had her and her family killed.

I lifted the wine glass to my lips.

"The Zetas will pay for what they did to her and her grandparents."

I choked on my wine. The Zetas? "But—"

"Señor Diaz, I'm sorry to interrupt but you need to see this." Yet another mustached man pointed a remote control at one of the walls. Panels slid away revealing a television set. The screen flickered, came to life, and filled with a shot of the resort I'd just left. I recognized the entrance. Were they reporting on my abduction?

The reporter spoke at an alarming rate—far faster than my ability to understand.

Why hadn't I learned Spanish?

The reporter stepped out of the shot, allowing the viewers a glimpse of two bodies piled by the front gate.

I had no difficulty making out a claw tattoo on the hand of the larger body on the screen.

Apparently Javier recognized Grizzly too. The stream of curses that escaped his lips was impressive—and I only understood one out of every ten words. His gaze shifted from the television to me. "Manuel!"

The medic appeared immediately.

"Take Señorita Fields back to her room." Javier's tone left no room for argument.

"This way." Manuel tried pulling my chair out.

I didn't move. "What's happening?"

"Those—" Javier let loose another string of curses "—Zetas. Do they think they can get away with this?"

"That's the man who abducted me." I pointed to the screen while everything I'd eaten roiled in my stomach. "The Zetas killed him? Why?"

Javier shifted his gaze to me.

His eyes weren't dead anymore. Something worse than death burned with cold fire in his irises.

Icicles formed in my veins. "I'll go now." I stood.

"Goodnight, Señorita Fields. Sleep well." Javier's voice was as a cold as his eyes.

I hurried my steps and followed Manuel down the endless hallway.

Manuel wasn't a big man. I retained enough of what I'd learned as a child to know I could knock him out.

But what then?

I couldn't run in an evening gown and four-inch heels. And where would I run? I didn't know where I was. There was no place to run.

I sighed.

"Are you still hungry?" asked Manuel. "I can have something sent from the kitchen."

"No." The sight of Grizzly's hand had stolen what little appetite I had. "But, thank you."

"Do you need ice for your wrist?"

"I'm fine."

We reached my room and he opened the door and waited for me to enter.

I paused, looked up into Manuel's face. "Why am I here?"

He returned my gaze. "I don't know, Señorita." He nodded toward the telephone. "If you need anything, just pick up the receiver."

"I need to go home."

He looked away. "They won't hurt you."

Neither one of us believed that.

# SIXTEEN

I paced the too pretty bedroom. An elegant cage was still a cage. And I was locked inside.

I threw myself on the fainting lounge in the closet, pulled off Javier's Jimmy Choos, and threw them at the wall.

I unzipped the Gucci gown, stepped out of it, and left it on the floor.

The bracelets I tossed onto the dresser.

The same with the earrings.

I paced in my underwear until it occurred to me there might be video cameras.

I stalked back to the closet and pulled on a pair of jodhpurs (the only pant option), an oversized cashmere sweater, and a pair of riding boots stiff with newness.

Then I paced some more.

I made mental lists—the mistakes I'd made in my life (over-plucking my eyebrows at thirteen, attending college in California within an hour of Chariss rather than heading east, dating Jake, and most of all coming to Mexico). I reviewed the reasons I should have dumped Jake months before he faked his death (he lied to me—daily). And I hatched a plan for escaping the hacienda but rejected it as suicidal.

In the movies, a kick-ass heroine might prevail against a gang of heavily armed men. In real life, the not-so-kick-ass woman would get herself shot. Or raped. Or both.

Back and forth.

If Javier was to be believed, the Zetas had killed Marta's family. Had she double-crossed them? Decided not to give them the drive?

They'd come looking for it. For her. And when she died without giving it to them, they decided I had it.

They'd come for me.

As had Javier.

How had he known where I'd be? The thought stopped me in my tracks.

Who knew I was leaving the hotel?

The better question was who didn't know.

The concierge knew. And Mike. And Brett. And probably half the lobby.

I growled at an innocent print of a Frida Kahlo painting and looked more closely. Not a print. An actual painting.

My cage was definitely gilded.

I paced over to the telephone, picked up the receiver, and held it to my ear while my pointer finger hovered above the dial. Who was I supposed to call?

"Good evening, Señorita Fields. How may I assist you?"

"I need some fresh air."

Silence.

"I mean it. I need air. Now. I can't breathe in this room." I gasped as if my lungs were failing me.

"Someone will be happy to escort you around the grounds tomorrow."

"I can't breathe." My voice pitched to somewhere between shriek and panic attack.

"I'm sorry, Señorita Fields, but—"

"Please. Just for a few minutes. Just open the doors to the veranda."

"I—"

"Please." I could sense the man at the end of the phone weakening. "I just need air. I'm desperate."

"I'll send someone."

And everyone said I couldn't act.

"Thank you. *Gracias*."

A few minutes later someone tapped on the door.

"Come in."

A man almost as big as Grizzly lumbered into my room. He gave me one short nod then crossed the expanse of carpet to the doors to the veranda, withdrew a keycard, and swiped a sensor.

Seconds later he swung open the doors and I stepped into the night air.

The veranda ran the length of the house with seating areas and fire pits and lounge chairs.

I took one very deep, very obvious breath then sank into a chair and put my feet on an ottoman.

Almost-Grizzly rested his hand on his gun and leaned against the side of the house.

We sat in silence.

I tried to get a sense of the landscape despite the darkness. That large building to the right had to be the stable—the one filled with Ignacio Quintero's prized Aztecas. But where was the road? Where were the lights from nearby houses? Thanks to the setting sun earlier in the day, I knew I faced west. Was that the best direction to run if I got the chance?

I saw darkness and stars. No road. No lights. No escape.

A cool breeze whistled through the trees and I shivered.

I stood. "I'm going to grab a blanket. I'll be right back."

I dashed inside, grabbed the throw that had been artfully draped across the bottom of the bed, and dashed back outside before Almost-Grizzly could lock me up again.

I chose a chaise, tucked the blanket around me, and stared at the darkness.

Almost-Grizzly did a fine job holding up the wall.

In the darkness, something roared.

"What's that?" I looked over my shoulder at Almost-Grizzly.

"One of the lions."

I swallowed. "Lions?"

"Sí. Señor Quintero keeps them as pets."

"Real lions? From Africa?"

Almost-Grizzly nodded and grinned—a feral grin.

I turned back to the heavy darkness and stared until my eyes grew heavy.

*Choo!*

"God bless you," I murmured.

*Thud!*

I looked over my shoulder again.

Almost-Grizzly lay on the stone pavers, surrounded by a growing pool of crimson.

He hadn't sneezed. That *choo* had been a silencer. My hands rose in the air of their own accord.

"It's okay, Poppy. It's me." A familiar voice filtered through the darkness.

I rose from my chaise. "How did you find me?"

"I put a tracker in your locket."

My hand rose to my throat. Stalker much? "You what?" Outrage made me louder than was safe.

"You heard me. Listen, I know you'd like to give me hell for that. But could you do it later? We need to get out of here."

Jake made an excellent point.

I looked back at poor Almost-Grizzly. "You killed him."

"He wasn't going to let you go."

"But you killed him."

"He was a *sicario* in the Sinaloa Cartel. He knew the risks."

"But you killed him."

"Could we talk about that later, too?" Jake's voice was that of a man being sorely tested.

I stepped into the darkness. "How are we getting out of here? Do you have a car?"

"Not exactly."

"What exactly do you have?"

"Feet. The rendezvous point is five miles to the west."

"A landing strip?"

"No. They'll be watching their landing strips. A clearing."

In the distance an animal roared.

"What was that?" Jake asked.

"Ignacio keeps lions."

"Oh." He swallowed. "I'm sure they're caged."

I wasn't. "We're escaping on foot? That's your plan? Seriously? We'll never make it." I looked down at my exceedingly new, exceedingly stiff boots. "They'll hunt us down."

"Of course we'll make it." There was the supremely confident Jake—the man who'd shattered my heart four times. Two break-ups, one death, and one Lazarus maneuver.

The *need* to punch him in the jaw tightened my hand into a fist. "We won't make it. Not on foot. Can you ride?"

"Of course."

"This way."

I led Jake to the stables.

He paused in the doorway and stared at the stalls. "Those are horses." A master of stating the obvious.

"That's generally what one finds in a stable."

"I thought you meant motorcycles."

"Because the roads up here are so good?"

He gulped. So much for all that confidence.

I read the horses' names on the front of the stalls, memorized two, and dashed into the tack room. There and there. I grabbed the horses' bridles and returned to the aisle. "Grab Maria."

"What?"

"The gray horse in the stall behind you."

"How?"

"Never mind." I slipped past Jake, petted Maria on the neck then slipped the bit into her mouth and the bridle over her head. Holding the reins, I led her out of the stall. "Hold these." I gave the reins to a very nervous looking Jake.

"Hey, Pablo," I crooned to the chestnut gelding in the next stall.

He nickered.

I slipped into the stall, put Pablo's bridle on him, and led him into the aisle.

"No saddles?" asked Jake.

"No." We didn't have time to adjust girths or stirrups or find the right saddle blankets. "Hold onto Pablo and I'll give you a leg up."

Jake just stared at me.

"Can you mount a horse without a boost?"

From Jake's expression, I was pretty sure the answer was no.

I laced my fingers together. "Step into my hands with your left foot and swing your right leg over Maria's back."

"Are you sure about this?"

"Positive."

Jake stepped into my hands and I hoisted him onto Maria. "You'll need these." I handed him the reins.

I took a second to rub Pablo's velvety nose, gathered the reins and part of his mane, and threw myself onto his back. "Let's go."

We rode out of the stable.

"Which way?" I asked.

"To the west."

"You already said that. I don't have a sense of direction up here. Which way?"

"Take a left."

We rode into the trees.

When we were at least a mile away from the hacienda—far from being overheard—

I straightened my spine and my shoulders, lifted my chin, and asked, "How could you?"

"How could I what?"

"Pick something."

"I don't know why you're mad. That tracker is the only reason I found you."

"Did you know I'd be abducted?"

Silence. Not a peep from the man on the horse behind me.

"I thought so."

"You were interacting with dangerous people! Why did you come to Mexico in the first place?"

"I came to Mexico to get over your death."

"So this is my fault?"

"Yes," I hissed.

"I did what I had to do."

"And how many people are dead?" I did a quick count. Marta, her grandparents, the man outside my door, the man in the desert, and the man on the veranda. Six. I was linked to six deaths. My fingers tightened on the reins and Pablo tossed his head at the increased pressure. "Sorry." I pet the horse's neck and loosened my grip.

"You're sorry?"

"I was talking to the horse. Why would I apologize to you?"

"A little gratitude might be nice. I did just rescue you."

I consciously kept my fingers loose and ground my teeth instead. "Let's not talk."

"Why not?"

"You work for a government agency. You could have gotten me out of Mexico. But you didn't. You do whatever is easiest for you."

"Skydiving into Ignacio Quintero's stronghold wasn't easy."

"For you? I bet it was. Plenty of adrenaline and you get to play the hero."

More silence.

Fine by me. Anything Jake said would probably be a lie.

"I am sorry."

No he wasn't.

"You could have just broken up with me like a normal person. You didn't have to fake your death."

"There are things you don't know."

More lies.

"I'm sorry." He actually sounded contrite. "Not a day has gone by that I haven't thought of you—haven't missed you."

*Lalalalala.* If my hands hadn't held reins, I'd have covered my ears.

"I mean it, Poppy. I've missed your smile, and the way you wrinkle your nose when you're annoyed with me, your beautiful blue eyes—"

"They're green."

"They're blue."

"I know what color they are. They're mine. And they're green."

"Blue-green."

"Green."

*Whoosh.*

Something flew at us. A bat?

Pablo reared.

I squeezed with my knees and leaned into his neck.

*"Ooomph."*

Apparently Jake and Maria parted ways. I gathered the reins and looked over my shoulder. Jake was on the ground and Maria was headed back to her stall.

"Are you all right?" I demanded.

Jake stood. Slowly. Rubbing his backside. "I'm fine."

"We can ride double." I really did not want him that close to me.

"I'll walk."

"Suit yourself."

He limped forward a few steps.

"You're hurt."

"Nothing I can't handle."

"At the rate you're going, we'll get there tomorrow afternoon."

I extended a hand and helped haul Jake onto Pablo's back.

Pablo danced a few steps at the added weight then settled.

"Why did the Sinaloans kidnap you?"

New topic? Perfect. "I'm pretty sure it has to do with Ignacio Quintero's giant obsession with my mother."

"That's it?" Jake's breath tickled my neck.

I stiffened. "That's it."

"I thought they knew about the flash drive."

We rode for a moment before the obvious question occurred to me. "How do you know about the flash drive?"

# SEVENTEEN

A beam sliced through the trees. The sudden brightness arrived with the deafening whir of rotors.

Pablo disapproved of both the light and the noise. Strongly disapproved.

The horse reared on its hind legs.

"Lean for—"

My warning came too late. Jake slipped off Pablo's backside.

And he dragged me with him.

Pablo left us at a canter.

Meanwhile, Jake and I played Twister on the forest floor.

For an instant, I saw us through a film director's lens. Two people who shouldn't be together but couldn't help themselves. Tangled Limbs. Tangled emotions. Screwball comedy.

Screwball comedies were dead. And if we didn't get moving, we might be too.

"I'm assuming your chopper wouldn't use searchlights."

"That wasn't mine. We're too far away." Jake's voice was grim.

"So Javier is looking for us."

"Javier? Where's Quintero?"

"Away. He's on his way back to Mexico. Javier said it would take two days for him to get here."

"Damn." Jake's voice was grimmer than before. "We'd better get up."

Neither of us moved. Even with a sharp stick poking my upper arm, there was comfort in closeness. In the familiar smell of hair. In the familiar scent of skin. In the way we'd always fit together seamlessly.

The helicopter circled and the beam cut five feet to our right.

"C'mon, Poppy. We need to move." Grimmest voice yet.

I pushed up. It wasn't my fault my elbow ended up in his stomach or that I slipped in my too-new boots.

*"Ooomph."*

"You say *oomph* a lot." Pointing that out was easier than apologizing.

"Saving you may leave permanent scars."

If I had hackles, they would have risen. "You? Scars? You should see what you did to my psyche."

"I told you I was sorry." He rose. Slowly. As if his bones ached. As if breathing wounded him.

"Are you hurt?"

"I don't have time to be hurt."

He limped forward toward a spot where the trees left no room for light.

I followed. "Where don't you have time to be hurt?"

"My knee and—" he winced "—I might have broken a rib."

"Lean on me."

"You couldn't possibly support me."

"Which one is your good knee?" I wanted to kick it.

"Right."

I draped his left arm over my shoulders. "Let's get moving."

We walked, slipping on the uneven ground, tripping on rocks, stumbling over roots.

The helicopter made a third pass and we froze. This time the beam of light cut fifteen feet to our left.

We didn't move until the sound of rotors faded.

Jake was sweating. I'd run with him on a baking hot beach without seeing a drop of perspiration. And now, on a chilly night lit only by stars and a wan moon, sweat dotted his forehead.

"Just how badly are you hurt?" I demanded. "I want an honest answer."

"Not bad." The pain had affected his lying skills.

"Uh-huh."

"I'll live. Let's talk about something else."

Fine. If that's how he wanted it. "How do you know about the flash drive?"

"Can we talk about that later?"

"No. Because, if we die tonight, I want to know before I close my eyes."

"I was sent to recruit you."

Not what I was expecting to hear. And not an answer to my question. "What?"

"You heard me."

We lurched forward a few more steps. "Recruit me for what?"

"Mérida."

"Why me?"

"It was thought you could get to Ignacio Quintero."

The little part of my heart that had remained whole through his death and resurrection disintegrated into dust. Jake and I had never been real. He'd never cared about me. I'd been a job.

"I couldn't do it. I couldn't put you in that much—" he paused and looked around the pitch-dark mountain "—this much danger." He tilted his head and looked up at the distant stars. "Do you understand who you're dealing with?"

"A drug lord."

He snorted softly. "Quintero buys a kilo of cocaine in Columbia for two thousand dollars. That same kilo is worth thirty-five thousand in Chicago, one hundred thousand if it's broken down into grams."

"Chicago?"

"The Sinaloans control ninety percent of the drug trade in Chicago."

I too looked at the stars. They were blurry so I swiped at my eyes.

"The Sinaloans—Quintero—make three billion dollars a year. They're not going to let anything or anyone interfere with that."

The weight of Jake's arm across my shoulders was suddenly too heavy. He'd spent months getting to know me and decided I wasn't up to the task. My already broken heart ached and I stumbled.

Maybe he was right.

Maybe I wasn't up to it.

All we had to do was walk. One step followed by another. Walk. And I couldn't do that without tripping. "You thought I couldn't handle Quintero?"

"That's not it." He shook his head and his free hand crossed his chest as if he could hold his rib in place. "I knew you could handle him. It was me."

"You?"

"I couldn't let you walk into danger. Quintero's a sociopath. Maybe even a psychopath."

"Shouldn't that decision have been mine?"

He grunted.

"Why did you fake your death?"

"A separate issue."

One I would return to if I got the chance. "None of this explains how you know about the drive."

Jake sighed as if he knew what was coming next. "Gonzales works for Mérida."

I took a single, deep breath. "Gonzales-who-wouldn't-return-my-passport Gonzales?"

"Yeah."

This very moment I could be sitting on the deck at my house in Malibu. I could be in New York negotiating a publishing contract. I could be in Paris drinking a café au lait. Instead, I was running away (stumbling away) from *sicarios*. "Why didn't you make him return my passport?"

"We disagreed about that."

I should hope so. Why hadn't Gonzales returned my passport? He had to have known I had nothing to do with any of the deaths at the resort. We inched forward in silence and the answer came to me. "Gonzales used me as bait."

Jake didn't answer.

"You knew. And you let him. That's why you put the tracker in my necklace." So much for keeping me safe. The only reason I didn't slip out from under Jake's arm and disappear into the night was because I had no place to go.

"There's a lot at stake."

"I know. Nuevo Laredo and Afghani heroin and another cartel war."

Jake snapped his head in my direction. "You read what was on the drive."

"Guilty." There was no point in mentioning that Mia and André had read it too.

"You told Gonzales you hadn't."

"I lied."

"But he believed you."

"And everyone says I can't act."

"You can't. Gonzales is an idiot." Furrows—visible even in

the dark—cut from the edges of Jake's nose to the thin line of his mouth. "People would kill for that information."

"I am aware." Dry. Bone dry. That was my tone. "Although, I don't see why. It doesn't take a rocket scientist to figure out that if the Zetas are weak the Sinaloans will go after Nuevo Laredo."

"That's not the dangerous part." Jake planted his feet. "Afghanis moving heroin through Mexico. That's the dangerous part. Hell." He shook his head. "You are in so much danger."

"If that's true, the best thing we can do is get out of here." I tugged at him.

"*Por aquí!*" A voice sliced through the darkness.

A bird that had settled in for the night squawked its displeasure. A bat whooshed by. The adrenaline surge in my veins gave me strength. I pulled Jake forward. "C'mon. We need to move." My voice was barely a whisper. "How far are we from the pick-up site?"

"Too far. And they're too close." He glanced in the direction the voice had come from. "We won't make it."

If sunny, always-too-confident Jake said we wouldn't make it, we wouldn't make it.

We.

"Can you make it by yourself?" I demanded.

A stubborn expression settled on his face. "I'm not leaving you."

"Then we both die."

His jaw dropped.

"Ignacio Quintero wants to meet me." I closed my eyes, blotting out Jake's face. "He wants to woo me. His men aren't going to hurt me."

"No. I'm not leaving you."

"What choice do we have?"

"We can make a stand."

Men could be such idiots. "In the dark? With one gun?

Against God knows how many *sicarios*? You need to go. I'll lead them in a different direction."

"Poppy." His voice was a plea.

"If you go, I'll convince them a Zeta snatched me."

"You're a terrible actress."

"I convinced Gonzales. Which way is the landing strip?"

Jake didn't move.

"We don't have time. Tell me." I slipped out from under his arm. "Which way?"

"But—"

"Which way, Jake?"

He pointed to our left.

"Next time you rescue me, bring backup." I stepped away from him, toward the voices. "Go!"

Jake gazed at me with an unreadable expression on his face.

"Go!"

Still he paused. "I'm sorry about this." Suddenly there was a knife in his hand and its blade was cutting into my skin.

Blood ran down my cheek. "What the hell?"

"I love you." He lurched into the trees—heading west.

I veered to the left—crashed to the left. Even with the handicap of my stiff boots, I'd be able to move faster than Jake could. If the *sicarios* followed a trail, it needed to be mine.

I trotted along in the dark. I made noise. I disturbed birds. I breathed in gasps.

There! Up ahead. The trees thinned and moonlight lit a clearing. I raced toward the light.

I emerged from the trees and found myself above a poppy field.

An enormous poppy field on the side of the mountain. It was a lovely scene. A field of moonlight-kissed flowers waving in the light breeze. Too pretty to be the source of so much misery.

I straightened my shoulders and formed a plan. Presumably the field required workers. There had to be a road. If I made it to the road, I might actually escape.

I paused, listened, and heard voices. Maybe. The soft whispers could have been the wind. I hoped the voices were following me and not Jake.

I took one small, tentative step toward the field and the ground gave way beneath my heel.

*"Eeeek!"* For half a second my arms spun like windmills searching for balance where there was none. I slid down the slope on my backside, legs akimbo, arms flailing, and landed in a heap. A shower of dirt and twigs and rocks followed me.

Could this night get any worse?

Had the *sicarios* heard me?

I hauled myself off the ground and dashed into the field, weaving my way through flowers that reached up to my hips. In addition to the flowers, there were stalks topped with odd bulbs. Sticky bulbs—almost gummy. *Yech!* Whatever sap was on them was nasty.

*Ch-ch-ch-ch-ch-ch.*

I turned in a circle looking for the source of the sound.

*Ch-ch-ch-ch-ch-ch—ssss.*

A stream of water cut across my chest, soaking my sweater.

I'd tempted fate by thinking the night couldn't get any worse. Who would have guessed that hidden poppy fields would be irrigated with automatic sprinklers?

Not me.

Shivering in the chill air, and quickly wet through, I slogged down the length of the field and found a dirt rut that might, if one's eyes were crossed after drinking a whole bottle of tequila, be called a road.

I followed the rut down and down and down until the dirt met a narrow lane. An actual road. Well, almost.

Down again.

Surely the road led to a town or—

I blinked, blinded by headlights.

The truck stopped and a man barked at me. "Hands up!"

Or that's what I assumed.

He might have said almost anything—his Spanish was too rapid for me to catch a single word. Sticking my hands in the air seemed the wisest course.

Under normal circumstances, I could charm most men. The circumstances weren't normal. I'd witnessed a murder, been thrown from a horse, slid down a mountain, and been doused by a sprinkler system meant for poppies. There were probably drowned rats that looked more attractive than I did. *"No hablo español. Hablas inglés?"*

A uniformed man with an automatic rifle stepped out from behind the lights.

*"Quién eres?"*

My name is Poppy Fields. *Mi nombre es Poppy Fields.* Are you police officers?"

Silence.

*"Son policías?"*

A man laughed. More than one man.

The creepy crawly feeling that ran down my spine was not a good sign.

I was an unprotected *gringa* in clothes that fit like a wet second skin wandering the forest.

"I was staying with Javier Diaz and I was kidnapped. Do you know Señor Diaz? Do you know Señor Quintero?"

The laughter stopped. The men had a quick, emphatic discussion.

Then one of them used his gun to motion me toward the back of the truck.

I held my hands up higher.

*"Rapido!"* The man gestured with his gun.

That gun—I was out of choices. I followed his instructions.

The back of the pick-up had recently been used to transport livestock. Goats?

My eyes watered but I didn't complain. I just hauled myself onto the truck bed.

Now I was wet, dirty, and smelled like a goat.

I wrapped my arms around my shins and rested my forehead against my knees.

One of the armed men climbed in after me.

With a bone-jarring lurch, the truck moved.

Hopefully, Javier would be glad to see me. Because that was where we were going. It had to be. We were headed up the mountain.

If he believed I'd been abducted by a Zeta, I had a chance. If he thought an American DEA agent had attempted my rescue, I was as good as dead. I practiced my story.

# EIGHTEEN

The man driving the truck must have called ahead because Javier was standing on the veranda in front of the hacienda when we arrived. A dark storm had gathered around his head and the thunder roared (or maybe that was the lions).

The night air, my wet clothes, and Javier's expression conspired to give me the shivers. I shook so badly the man with the gun lowered his weapon and helped me out of the truck.

"What happened?" Javier's voice was as cold as the wind cutting through my sweater.

He wanted an explanation now? Here? In the drive? I was freezing and I hadn't had enough time to rehearse.

Chariss always said acting was about mining one's soul, borrowing real emotion, and using those feeling for a character.

My character was a traumatized woman. A woman about to break. A woman deserving of sympathy.

I needed tears. That was easy. I thought about Jake. I thought about how deeply he'd wounded me, how he'd lied, and how he'd used me. I thought about him not making it to the pick-up site and dying (for real) alone in the mountains of Sinaloa.

My eyes were awash with tears. "I was sitting on the veranda and someone shot your guard."

"Who?" Javier demanded.

"A man. He didn't tell me his name."

"What did he look like?"

A circle of stone-faced *sicarios* watched Javier interrogate me. Their hands rested on their guns as if they'd start shooting any second now. A few spit on the ground near their feet—near my feet. Others shifted from side to side—edgy. They were ready to avenge their comrade.

I covered my mouth with a shaking hand and looked at the men. "He looked like them. "Jeans, boots, mustache, and a gun."

A few of the men grumbled.

"You spoke to him," said Javier. "In what language?"

"Spanish and English. My Spanish is bad. His English was worse."

"Where were you going?"

"He said something about an airplane."

"You were going to the landing strip?"

I thought about the man with the Glock in my ribs, his eyes staring sightlessly at the Baja sky, and my certainty I'd be next. I used that terror. "I was s-s-so frightened. I don't know. Maybe."

"You stole horses."

I stood silent—letting the moment stretch. Tears coursed down my cheeks and I crossed my arms over my chest. "He stole the horses. He had a gun. I thought he'd shoot me."

"But, he didn't."

"No. But he—" my voice broke as if what came next was too terrible to say aloud "—he touched me. He said he was going to enjoy having Quintero's woman."

A few of the *sicarios* muttered.

"But you went with him," said Javier.

I gulped. "If I didn't go with him he'd shoot me."

Javier crossed his arms over his chest. He wasn't buying my story.

"I fell off my horse at the first opportunity. I thought being on foot would slow us down." I gazed up through my tangled hair at Javier's impassive face. "I thought you might be looking for me. Maybe following us."

His lips thinned. "Then what happened?"

"He put me on the second horse." My voice hitched. "He said I walked too slow. When I fell off the second horse, he hit me." I rubbed my collarbone where a sapling had whacked me on my fall down the mountain.

Javier's expression darkened. Did he believe me?

"He dragged me along but I kept slipping and falling." I looked down at the too-new boots (now muddied and scratched and water-stained). "Then we heard voices. I prayed it was you and your men and I dragged my steps."

One of the *sicarios* cracked each of his knuckles. *Pop, pop, pop.*

I swallowed (hard) and continued, "When I was certain I heard voices, I pulled my arm free and ran for a break in the trees. I ran—" I paused and gauged my audience. The *sicarios'* eyes might be dead but their foreheads were wrinkled in concern. "I ran until the ground fell away."

Javier snorted.

Was he buying this? My life hung in the balance. I had to convince Javier. My character needed honesty. I thought about my dad. "I was unconscious for a few minutes. When I woke up I was in a poppy field. I figured there had to be a road somewhere, so I walked until I found one. Then—" I pointed "—those men picked me up. I told them your name and Señor Quintero's and they brought me here."

Javier spoke in rapid Spanish to the uniformed men.

They nodded.

No one looked pleased I'd been rescued.

Somewhere nearby, a lion roared.

Javier stared at me with considering eyes.

Was I about to be given to the *sicarios* for their evening entertainment? Fed to the lions?

A sob escaped my chest—a sob that encompassed six dead people, a knife at my throat, a gun in my ribs, Jake's parting words, and the blisters on my feet. I sank to the ground and buried my head in my hands.

Too much? I peeked through my fingers.

Javier was speaking fast and low to Manuel.

Too fast and too low for me to catch a single word.

I reached up to my throat, needing the comfort of my locket. My neck was bare.

Somewhere in those miles of mountain terrain, I'd lost my father's last gift to me.

Fresh tears—real ones—welled in my eyes. I lowered my head and sobbed.

If Javier moved me from this house, Jake wouldn't be able to find me.

If Javier suspected I was complicit in the escape attempt, he wouldn't find Jake's tracker.

I moaned as if I was in pain. That was easy. I was.

Manuel stepped toward me and extended his hand. "Senorita Fields."

I pushed my wet hair away from my face and stared up at him. Had I convinced them?

"Ay!" He jumped back as if I was a poisonous snake who'd suddenly appeared in his path.

What? What had I done?

Manuel pointed at my face. "Zetas!"

Javier bounded off the veranda and grabbed my chin in his hand. His eyes searched my eyes, my face. Then, with his free hand, he traced a Z on my cheek. "You didn't say anything about a knife."

Oh. That. "I was more worried about the gun."

Javier gave the *sicarios* rapid instructions.

A few of the men peered at my face and muttered, "*Zetas.*" The rest hurried toward parked vehicles.

If I'd only spotted those vehicles when I arrived, Jake and I could have stolen one and I wouldn't be in this mess.

"Let me help you up." Manuel lifted me off the ground and gave me his arm.

With Javier watching, we limped toward the house.

"Señorita Fields." Javier's voice stopped us.

I looked over my shoulder at him. The storm clouds were still there.

"I am glad you are back with us. The man who took you from us will pay."

I simply nodded.

And people said I couldn't act.

---

MANUEL LED me back to my bedroom. "How badly are you hurt?"

I barely managed a shrug.

"I will give you time to wash, then I will be back."

Manuel didn't want to examine a filthy, wet woman who smelled like a goat? Imagine that.

I nodded once.

He left me.

Numb. I felt numb.

Numbly, I turned on the gold taps in the sunken tub.

Numbly, I stripped off the ruined clothes.

Numbly, I examined my bruised and bloody body in the mirror.

I turned off the bathtub taps (I couldn't soak in blood) and stepped into the shower where I turned on the water as hot as

I could bear, watched my blood circle the drain, and felt numb.

I shampooed. I conditioned. I loofahed.

And when I was clean, I stepped out of the shower, sank into the bathtub, and let the hot water melt away the physical pain.

I rested the back of my head against the lip of the tub and closed my eyes.

Where was Jake? Had he made it to the pick-up site?

I'd done everything I could to make sure he got away.

Would he come back for me?

Was I still bait?

Tears wet my face, burned Jake's cut on my cheek, and salted the bath water.

When my fingertips puckered, I stood and wrapped myself in a fluffy bath sheet.

My bottom and lower back ached. My collar bone outright hurt. There were bruises all over my body. My feet were a mess of blisters. And my face—I avoided looking in the mirror.

Hopefully Jake's mark wouldn't scar.

"Señorita Fields?"

Manny had returned.

"Give me a minute." I slipped into the La Perla pajamas Javier had provided, pulled on a robe, and emerged from the bathroom. "Is there someone who can throw those clothes away?"

Manuel nodded, picked up the ruined jods, sweater, and underthings with the tips of his fingers, and tossed them into the hall outside my room. "They smell."

He didn't have to tell me.

"Like a goat." I wrinkled my nose. "Someone transported livestock in that truck."

"*Muy apestoso.*"

I had no idea what that meant but I smiled at him.

He smiled back. A shy smile with a hint of gentleness. "Let's check you out, then you can go to bed."

I glanced at the veranda where Almost-Grizzly's body had fallen.

"Do not worry. Señor Diaz has tripled the patrols. You will be safe."

I was more worried about seeing a pool of blood.

Manuel had antiseptic cream for my cuts and blisters. He tsked over a few of my bruises but there wasn't anything he could do to treat them. "The good news is nothing is broken. The best thing for you is sleep. I will check on you in the morning."

I crawled into bed certain I'd spend the rest of the night staring at the ceiling.

Apparently murder, kidnapping, and failed rescues take a lot out of a woman. I slept till noon, stretched, and realized I was starving.

I picked up the phone on the bedside table. "Hello?"

"*Buenos días.*"

"May I have something to eat?" My stomach rumbled. "Please?"

"*Si.*"

I hung up the phone and stumbled into the bathroom where the mirror showed me my face and the red Z on my cheek.

Even if the cut did scar, I couldn't complain. In the clear light of a new day, I knew the cut had probably saved my life.

A few minutes later, someone tapped at the door.

"Come in."

A plaid-shirted *sicario* wheeled in a silver cart filled to near collapse with covered dishes. There was bacon and scrambled eggs and warm tortillas. There were sliced avocados, salsa, fresh fruit, and an enormous tray of pastries. Best of all, there was a pot of coffee and cream.

"*Gracias.*" The word couldn't adequately convey my gratitude.

"*De nada.*" He left me with enough food for ten people.

I helped myself to eggs and bacon and a cup of coffee.

*Scritch, scritch.*

"What in the world?"

*Scritch, scritch.*

Certain it was locked, I tried the door to the hallway. It opened easily and Consuela raced into my room.

*Yip.* She pulled back her lips and showed me her teeth.

"No." Calm and firm—that was the way to handle dogs.

Consuela snarled at me.

"No."

Consuela's buggy-eyes bugged a bit more.

Had no one ever told her no?

*Grrrr.*

"No."

Consuela sat down on her petite haunches and looked at me—considering.

"Do you want a bite of bacon?" I asked.

Apparently bacon transcended our language barrier and her dislike of women and strangers. Her tail wagged.

I broke off part of a slice, gave it to the little dog, and resumed my brunch.

*Yip.* Consuela looked up at me expectantly.

"One more bite. Too much will make you sick."

I finished my meal with Consuela curled at my feet then changed into one of the dresses Javier had selected for me. Grecian in cut, it flowed loosely around me, showing off every bruise on my arms and collar bone. The shoes weren't happening—not with my blisters.

I padded back to the telephone. "Thank you for breakfast. Would someone please come get the cart?"

"*Sí, Señorita.*"

I settled onto one of the club chairs to wait. Consuela settled onto my lap.

*Knock, knock.*

Consuela's ears perked but she didn't move.

"Come in," I called.

The man who'd come to collect the cart saw Consuela on my lap, paled, and crossed himself. "*Madre de Dios.*"

Consuela growled at him.

"Shhhh," I told her. "That's not nice." Then I turned to the man. Was wearing a plaid shirt a condition of employment? A uniform? "Please, leave the coffee."

"*Sí.*" With one eye on Consuela, he collected everything but my cup, the coffee pot, and the cream, then scuttled out into the hallway.

When the door clicked shut, I scratched behind Consuela's ears. "What did you do to scare these men so badly?" I lowered my voice to a whisper. "I need your secrets."

# NINETEEN

*Knock, knock.*

The door to the bedroom opened before I could respond.

Good thing I wasn't naked because Javier entered without an invitation. He wore a charcoal gray suit. In the cream and white bedroom, he was a slash of darkness. "I had to see this for myself. That dog won't tolerate anyone but Ignacio."

Consuela, who was curled in my lap like a cat, drew her lips back and snarled.

He snorted softly. "See what I mean?"

I scratched behind her ears. "She's just misunderstood."

Javier crossed the room. He stood too near my chair. He loomed over me. "Did you bribe her?"

"Of course not."

Consuela burped.

"Did you give her some of your breakfast?"

"No." I lowered my face to Consuela's and she licked my nose with her little pink tongue.

The twist of his lips said he didn't believe me. "Are you feeling better today?"

"I am." I touched my marked cheek. "Thank you for asking."

"Have you remembered anything more about the man who abducted you and killed Joaquim?" A woman could cut herself on the edge in Javier's voice. "That Zeta?"

"No." The key to a successful lie was keeping it simple. If I embellished my story, I'd get caught.

"I find it amazing the Zetas knew you'd be here."

"Where else would you hide me?" I kept my tone mild and looked up at him with Chariss's best innocent expression.

"Ignacio has other houses."

"Maybe they sent people to those houses too."

Javier's lip curled. "Yes. But why did they want you so badly? An infiltration into the heart of Sinaloa was an enormous risk."

The man didn't believe me. He hadn't believed me last night. Or had he? Did he know about the drive?

My hand, petting the little dog in my lap, froze.

Why was I still alive?

"Such a mystery." He took the chair across from mine. "I'm glad your injuries weren't more serious. Manuel tells me aside from the cut on your face you suffered nothing more than a few bruises and blisters." He shifted his gaze to my bare feet. "You are very lucky."

"Lucky? That's not the term I'd use."

"You wouldn't?" Did he mean I was lucky he hadn't handed me over for a gang rape before cutting off my head? Or perhaps he meant I was lucky Ignacio Quintero wanted me alive. For now.

I cleared my throat. "Lucky would be sitting on the terrace of my house in Malibu without a single thought about murder or kidnapping or cartels."

"I'm sure after you spend a few days with Ignacio, the thought of home will seem even sweeter."

What the hell did that mean?

Consuela lifted her head and growled.

"I must know, if you didn't bribe her, how did you win over the dog?"

"I grew up with dogs."

"So did every man here."

"Well, maybe she really does like women."

He shrugged. "She's nothing but trouble. If it were up to me, I'd feed her to the lions." Was he talking about Consuela or me?

"But Señor Quintero loves her. You told me so yourself." I leaned down and kissed the top of Consuela's head. "If Señor Quintero decides he doesn't want her, I'd be happy to take her home with me."

"Right now, he does want her." Darkness emanated from Javier, dimming even the sunbeams shafting through the glass doors. "And you are right, until he changes his mind, she is safe."

Games. What game was Javier playing?

Was he telling me I was safe as long as I pleased Quintero? When Quintero's protection was gone, I was lion food? Was I being paranoid?

We needed a new topic. Fast. "You offered to show me the house. Do you have time this afternoon?"

"I will leave that pleasure for Ignacio."

I sighed as if not touring the house was a major disappointment. "It's probably just as well." I added another sigh. "I can't wear shoes."

"Ah, yes—your injuries."

"They're very painful."

"I'm sure."

"Does Señor Quintero have a library?"

"The books are in Spanish."

"A media room?"

"If that will keep you entertained."

"It will."

"Because we don't want you getting restless again."

"No. We don't."

"I'll take you there now."

"Thank you." I tucked Consuela into my arms and stood.

Javier led me back to the foyer, through the living room where the sicario had tipped the couch, and into a screening room worthy of a Hollywood mogul. Its leather seats were enormous and probably moved and vibrated in conjunction with the action on the screen. Gilded columns held up a ceiling painted like the night sky, and heavy gold curtains were tied back to the edges of a massive screen. Framed movie posters—all of Chariss's biggest hits—covered the walls.

"This button is for the film library." Javier's lips quirked and he handed me a remote. "That button is for the television."

"Thank you."

"I want you to enjoy your time here." He made the mundane pronouncement sound like a threat.

"I appreciate that."

He left me alone with Consuela and a screen the size of two SUVs.

I sat, settled the dog on my lap, and flipped on the television.

My face greeted me. Then the screen cut to Chariss, who appeared in front of the Ritz Paris. Tears stood in her eyes. If I didn't know better, I'd have thought they were real. "Please," she begged. "Return Poppy safely."

I couldn't argue that.

A Spanish-speaking reporter said something I couldn't understand then James Ballester's face filled the giant screen. "Poppy was scared. An actress of her acquaintance had already died and she just wanted to go home. The Mexican authorities wouldn't let her. They held her passport. Now this horrible thing has happened." He glared at the camera. "I blame the authorities." His expression softened to the soulful look. "Poppy, if you can hear this, we love you and we're doing everything possible to get you back."

My throat swelled with unspent emotion. My blood chilled with dread.

James meant wel,l but antagonizing the Mexican government and men like Agent Gonzales wouldn't help get me home.

The screen cut to a photograph of Marta Vargas followed by pictures of her grandparents. Then came video of the crumpled Jeep, the Escalade, and medics loading Juan into an ambulance.

I froze the screen.

I was big news.

I stared at that Escalade. Stared and thought.

Why hadn't Javier simply put one of his people behind the wheel of that SUV? I wouldn't have questioned a man who showed up in a hotel shirt. I'd have climbed into the vehicle and been abducted without the accident or the murdered *sicario* or the fuss.

No one would know what had happened to me—a famous-for-being-famous woman disappeared without a trace. Depending upon her schedule, Chariss might push and keep the story in the news for a few weeks. After that, I'd get an episode on *48 Hours*, then I'd be forgotten.

Instead, Javier had left bread crumbs. The ruined Jeep. The body. The driver left alive with a description of the helicopter.

Javier had wanted a fuss. Why?

With all this fuss, could Ignacio afford to let me go? Did a man who murdered people, laundered billions of dollars, and produced untold amounts of heroin care about a kidnapping charge? Hopefully not.

Consuela lifted her head, sniffed, and jumped off my lap.

"Where are you going?"

She trotted to a closed door then turned and looked at me expectantly. *Yip.*

"It's not my house." I had a feeling opening the wrong door in Ignacio's hacienda would be a lot like opening the door to Bluebeard's closet.

Consuela did not share my concern. *Yip.*

"We could watch a movie."

Consuela rolled her eyes. *Yip.*

"Fine," I huffed. Then, per her instructions, I stood.

*Yip, yip.* The doggy equivalent of *hurry up.*

I closed my hand around the knob and the door opened easily. *Whew!* Bluebeard's closet would be locked. I was sure of it.

Consuela dashed into the room on the other side.

I peered after her.

The room was a shrine to Chariss. Photographs of her papered the walls. Glass boxes held props from her movies— the necklace she'd worn in *Body Language,* the hat she wore in the ill-considered remake of *My Fair Lady*, the shoes she wore in *The Stiletto Gang.*

I tiptoed inside. The room smelled of Creed Fleurissimo, the perfume Chariss always wore (*if it's good enough for Grace Kelly to wear on her wedding day, it's good enough for me*). I breathed deeply. Not that Chariss's scent was a comfort but the rest of the house, despite its elegance, smelled of too many men.

With a satisfied grunt, Consuela hopped up onto a dog bed that had to have cost more than ten thousand dollars. There was a cherub—a cherub larger than Consuela—and the entire frame was covered in gold crystals and pearls. The little dog settled onto a shearling pillow and watched me with one eye.

The dog bed, along with the desk and its chair, were the only pieces of furniture in the room.

Somehow, I shifted my gaze from the monstrosity of Consuela's bed and studied the pictures on the wall— photographs taken on movie sets, at awards shows, by paparazzi. There were even a few of Chariss and me together. Brittle smiles, tight eyes, stiff spines.

"Wow." I sat down behind the desk. "He really does have a thing for Chariss."

He'd collected all manner of Chariss-related items. Now he'd collected me.

There were even framed photographs on the desk. I picked up a silver frame and looked at the picture within. Chariss and—oh, wow.

When had my mother been photographed with Ignacio Quintero? It seemed unlikely their paths would cross. Yet, there they were—smiling happily.

It had to have been a photo-op—just like those pictures with me and Marta. Or photo-shop. I squinted. Ignacio's head looked as if it belonged on his body. A real photo.

Wow.

I put the picture back on the desk.

*Ka-ka-shoo, ka-ka-shoo.* Consuela snored softly.

This room—Chariss's scent, the pictures, Consuela's bed—it had to be Ignacio's private retreat.

If Jake and the cavalry did come riding in to save me, it would be nice to repay them with actionable information.

I glanced at the door then slid the desk drawer open—just a few inches.

Another quick glance at the door.

A few more inches.

My heartbeat rang in my ears and my hands shook. I wasn't cut out for espionage.

One last glance door-ward.

A few more inches.

I peered inside.

A map of the U.S. and Mexican border covered the bottom of the drawer. Cities were circled in red pen—Tijuana, Nogales, Juarez, and Nuevo Laredo. In between the cities, there were smaller circles. All the legal border crossings neatly marked. And then there were gold stars in odd places. Illegal border crossings? I wished for my cellphone and the ability to take photos.

Consuela grumbled in her sleep and I jumped three feet out of my chair.

When my hands stopped shaking, I slid the drawer closed.

I wasn't an artist, there was no way I'd remember the details of that map. And, somehow, I doubted Jake and the people he worked with cared all that much about illegal entry points. They didn't want to arrest drug mules; they wanted to bring down drug lords. Like Quintero.

I sighed and picked up the picture of Chariss and Ignacio Quintero.

Where in the world had it been taken?

The dress Chariss was wearing—at least three seasons old. Cannes?

I put the frame down.

Too hard.

Consuela jumped, cast me a reproachful stare, then closed her eyes again.

Consuela was the least of my problems; I'd broken the frame. A tiny piece now stuck out at an odd angle.

I picked up the photo (Chariss and Ignacio still grinned) and pushed at the bit of silver sticking out of the side. Instead of slotting back into place, the bottom of the frame slid open and a rolled piece of paper fell out.

Again I glanced toward the door then with suddenly clumsy fingers I opened the little scroll. There were numbers. Routing numbers. Account numbers. Passwords. The kind of information that would make saving me worthwhile.

I looked around for a pen or a piece of paper.

Nothing.

If Ignacio found his account list missing, I'd be lion food.

But Jake and the people he worked with might be able to

make a real difference in the war on drugs if they could seize Quintero's cash. I needed those numbers.

All I had to do was locate a pen and paper, get back into this room, figure out how to open the frame again, copy everything down, then hide my notes.

Even in her sleep, Consuela snickered.

# TWENTY

A stiff-spined Javier sat across the dinner table from me. The man looked like a walking billboard for good genes and bespoke suits. What did the cowboy-booted, plaid-shirted *sicarios* think of his fine clothing?

Last night, he'd seemed set on impressing me, tonight he ignored me.

"I saw my mother on the television," I said. "On the news. She was crying."

Javier didn't even acknowledge he'd heard me.

"I was wondering if I could e-mail her and tell her I'm safe."

He looked up from his plate. "No. E-mails can be traced."

"What if I wrote a letter? Someone could mail it?"

"A letter?"

I nodded with enthusiasm. "You know, pen, paper, envelope, stamp—a letter." I played my trump card. "I'm sure Señor Quintero wouldn't want her to worry."

Javier glanced toward the ceiling. Not exactly an eye-roll —but close. "Fine."

"Maybe I could write it tonight."

Javier looked up from his tamales. "Fine."

"I'll need paper and a pen."

"Fine."

We ate a few bites in silence.

"That's quite a video library." Ignacio Quintero's video library consisted of every episode of every television show Chariss had ever been in, plus every movie she'd ever made. Nothing else.

"I thought you'd enjoy it." The man was a sadist.

"I think he has a few movies I haven't seen." I'd actually watched a few episodes of *The Smiths* and looked for Irene Vargas. I'd also searched Chariss's face for a hint of fear or uncertainty and saw only a woman sure of her beauty. Irene Vargas might have believed Chariss was insecure or frightened. I wasn't buying it. Not for a second. "I don't suppose I could watch them tomorrow?"

"Ignacio arrives tomorrow."

I had to move fast! I took a large sip of wine. "What time?"

"Around two."

"I'll watch a movie in the morning."

"You mean you don't sleep till noon every day?" An innocuous sentence. A charming man could have made it flirty. Javier made it mean.

"Only after being abducted." I smiled sweetly. If Jake came tonight, we'd have to find a way to steal that frame. If Jake didn't come, I'd make sure I had the information before I left this place. Javier wouldn't get away with kidnapping me.

"I've been thinking about that abduction." Javier's voice was chilly.

"What about it?"

"Your abductor didn't have much of a plan to get you out."

"No," I agreed. "He didn't. The entire attempt was half-assed." Typical of Jake to lead with his heart and not his head.

"The Zetas are former military operatives. They plan with

precision." Like planning a crash on a deserted toll road, three *sicarios*, and a helicopter.

I blinked and fluffed my hair. "I read the Zetas were in disarray and different factions were struggling for power."

Javier grunted.

"Maybe it was one of those factions that abducted me."

"Why abduct you?"

"Ransom? Extortion? The man who took me could have been working for one of the factions I read about."

Javier rubbed his chin. "Where did you do all this reading?"

In a file stolen from a Sinaloa Cartel computer. "I don't know. I think I saw a documentary, too. I don't remember."

We returned our attention to our meals. More silence. Itchy silence.

"This is pretty china."

"Ignacio's first wife picked it out."

I looked up from my plate. "He was married?"

Javier looked up too. "He *is* married. The third Señora Quintero lives in Culiacan."

How did Señora Quintero feel about her husband's obsession with Chariss? How would she react to my presence? My fork scraped against my plate. "How did you come to work for Señor Quintero?"

"He needed a CFO and I needed a job."

"Most men with MBAs are looking for a C-level job at a Fortune 500 company, not—"

"Not with a drug trafficker?" For an instant something akin to warmth lit Javier's eyes. "This organization grosses more money than any Fortune 500 company out there and our margins are better. If Ignacio would implement a few of my ideas, he could rule the world."

Perhaps realizing he'd tilted his hand a bit too far, Javier added, "Ignacio is making changes. And change should be incremental."

If that's what he told himself, I wasn't about to argue.

"Sometimes..." Javier stared at the picture of Chariss. Whoever he was talking to, it wasn't me. "Sometimes changes can be too big, too fast."

"Too big?"

He swung his gaze my way. Any warmth that had been in his eyes was frozen over. "Changing a business model too quickly can have unintended consequences."

Javier and Ignacio disagreed about something. Something big. Afghani heroin?

If the two men engaged in a battle for control of the Sinaloa Cartel, the hacienda was the last place I wanted to be.

Javier put down his fork and wiped his mouth with a napkin. "Please excuse me, I have work to do." He stood and flicked an invisible bit of lint off the arm of his jacket.

"The writing materials?" I looked up at him with wide eyes.

"Pick up your house phone and ask for them."

Flipping a spoonful of salsa at his snow-white shirt would be wrong. Dreadfully wrong. Besides, he was wearing an Hermés tie. Besides, he'd probably feed me to the lions.

Later that night, having acquired paper and pen, I sat down at the table in my room and wrote.

*Dear Mom* (I never called Chariss *Mom*—she'd know immediately something was off),

*I just wanted to let you know the people who took me are treating me well.*

*It's like you always say, I should be starring in a thriller* (Chariss had identified screwball comedies as my best genre). *Now I am.*

*Of course, I want to go home. There's no place like Beverly Hills* (I hadn't lived in Beverly Hills since I left for college). *I am hopeful they will let me go. Soon.*

*Love, Poppy*

I addressed the envelope to Chariss in care of Ruth

Gardner at Gardner, Jackson & Bray, stood, and stretched my back. Javier would read the letter before it was mailed (if it was mailed) but the point had never been the letter. The point had been a believable reason to ask for paper and a pen.

Consuela, who'd decided she was my new roommate, lifted her head from her paws and watched me walk over to the locked veranda doors.

I stared out into the night.

What if Jake hadn't made it?

What if he had, and the people he worked with decided I wasn't worth saving?

What if I was alone?

I crossed my arms over my chest. Did I have a hope of making it home?

Consuela rubbed her little head against my leg and I bent and picked her up. She still smelled of Chariss's perfume.

How often had Chariss accused me of floating through life?

Now, faced with the real possibility of my life ending, I saw her point. I wanted that accumulation of days and weeks and months and years to mean something. When I died, I wanted someone other than my personal shopper and a few paparazzi to know I'd lived.

"I don't mean fame," I whispered to Consuela. "I want to make a difference."

Consuela yawned.

Bringing down a drug cartel would make a difference. Even if Jake didn't come, if I could somehow escape with those account numbers, I had a real opportunity to damage the Sinaloa Cartel. For the rest of my life, I'd know I'd done something meaningful.

---

THE NEXT MORNING, I called for breakfast early.

The same *sicario* (different plaid shirt) wheeled in the same cart loaded with the same food (enough for an army).

I ate eggs, drank two cups of coffee, and sneaked tiny bites of bacon to Consuela. Then I showered, dressed, and picked up the house phone. "I've finished breakfast. Could someone come and get the cart. Also, I'd like to watch a movie. Would someone please take me to the theater?"

Two *sicarios* arrived at my door.

"This way," said the scarier of the two. A scar split his left cheek. A tattooed knife marked his right.

"*Gracias.*" Clutching Consuela tighter than was strictly necessary, I followed him. The roll of paper I'd concealed in my bra poked my breast. A minor annoyance compared to the pen (hidden in the waistband of my panties) trying to impale my lower back.

I sighed when we reached the theater.

The *sicario's* brows rose.

"Such a pretty room."

He shrugged (maybe he wasn't a Chariss Carlton fan), picked up the remote, and handed it to me.

Consuela snapped at him. He snatched his fingers away and took a giant step backward.

"Thank you. *Gracias.*" I turned on the screen just in time to see my face blown up to the size of two SUVs. No one's pores should ever look that big. Ever.

The reporter on the screen spoke in rapid Spanish.

Not for the first time (this week), I regretted choosing French as my foreign language in high school. Chariss had convinced me I'd learn Spanish by osmosis, and she was dating a French director, and pleasing her had been my priority. Turns out I couldn't learn a language just by hearing it spoken around me. The French director lasted less than two years.

Consuela and I settled into one of the seats and stared at the screen.

With his gaze fixed on the dog in my lap, our guide backed out of the theater.

On the screen, the shot switched to Chariss. Reporters surrounded her. She appeared to be outside LAX airport. I rubbed my eyes. Blinked. She was definitely at LAX. And Ruth Gardner stood at her side. Chariss had left a shoot? For me?

Someone must have told her it would look awful if she continued working when her only child had been kidnapped. Probably Ruth.

Chariss posed with pale cheeks, enormous eyes, and slightly (artfully) messy hair. She clasped her hands to her chest. She stared at the flashing cameras as if they were strangers. She was the very picture of a mother racked with worry.

It was Ruth who spoke. "Ms. Carlton is devastated by the abduction of her daughter and is committed to doing whatever is necessary to bring Poppy safely home. Poppy, if you can hear this, we're searching for you."

My throat swelled and I blinked back tears.

The reporters yelled out question after question.

"No," said Ruth. "We don't know who's holding her."

I wiped away a tear.

Ruth withstood another barrage of questions.

"Is it unsafe for Americans to travel in Mexico?" yelled the loudest reporter.

Ruth allowed herself a tiny, ironic smile. "No comment."

The Mexican reporter and her rapid Spanish filled the screen and I switched over to one of Chariss's early movies.

Ten minutes in, Consuela yawned and jumped off my lap.

Good dog.

She scratched against the door to Ignacio's retreat.

Better dog.

I abandoned my chair and let her in. She trotted to her over-the-top bed.

The air in the room hadn't changed a whiff. It was still scented with Fleurissimo.

The photograph still rested on the desk. Chariss and Ignacio still smiled brightly.

I extracted the pen and the roll of paper and sat.

Just sitting in Ignacio's chair raised my heart rate by twenty or thirty beats per minute.

I didn't have to do this. No one would ever know I'd been too scared to copy down a few account numbers.

No one but me.

I'd know.

I put the pen and paper down on the desk, glanced at the empty theater, and poked at the frame. The list fell into my waiting palm.

Another glance.

I wrote. The numbers were tiny. There were so many of them. And they were only useful if they were correct.

My hands shook. My palms slicked with sweat.

Was that a four or a nine? If I couldn't read my writing, it was a sure bet no one else could.

I shifted my gaze to the empty theater, wiped my hands on my skirt, took a deep breath, and wrote another line. Clearly.

Five more to go.

I snuck another look at the door. Was it possible for a human heart to explode? I paused and held my hand against my chest.

Two lines to go.

*Yip!*

My body lifted three feet in the air.

Consuela was chasing something in her sleep—her little legs ran and her nose twitched. What did a Chihuahua chase? Mice?

With a shaking hand, I finished the last line, rolled up

Ignacio's list, and returned it to its frame. Then I rolled up my list and slipped it into my bra.

"What are you doing in here?" Javier stood in the doorway.

"Consuela wanted to come." My hand shook too hard to wave at the little dog in her blinged-out bed. "I just had to sit down and take it all in."

"I told you he was a fan." Javier narrowed his eyes and rubbed his chin. "This is a private room."

Gulp. "I didn't think he'd mind and Consuela wanted her bed."

The pen on the desk was hidden by my forearm. Explaining that pen might prove difficult.

With my free hand, I picked up the photo of Chariss and Ignacio. "Where was this taken?"

"Cannes."

I'd been right. I replaced the photo and shifted my gaze to Consuela's bed. "Wherever did he find that?"

Javier's gaze shifted to Consuela and her pearl and Swarovski-studded resting place.

With a swipe of my arm, I knocked the pen into my lap.

"It's custom-made. No expense spared."

"Consuela seems to like it." Now that the pen was out of sight, I breathed easier. I pushed it into the seam where the seat met the back of the chair.

Javier returned his cold gaze to me. "Ignacio will be here in time for lunch. You should get ready."

Presumably that meant more than a messy bun and a make-up free face.

I stood. "Of course."

Again Javier's eyes narrowed, as if he knew I was up to something but couldn't figure out what.

I lifted my chin and swanned past him, all too aware of the paper biting into my breast.

He caught my arm, stopping me. "I'd advise you to say out of this room."

"Of course." My voice remained steady. Two syllables steady. No more. I shifted my gaze to the spot where his hand held my arm.

Dangerous sparks arced between us.

"Ouch!" Javier released me.

Consuela was at our feet and she had bitten through the fine wool of Javier's suit and embedded her teeth in his calf.

He kicked. Repeatedly.

A growling Consuela held on.

"Are you sure you want to kick Señor Quintero's pride and joy across the room?"

If looks could kill, I'd be dead—but Javier stopped kicking.

"Consuela," I crooned. "Let go."

The little dog rolled her eyes. Apparently she'd been aching to sink her teeth into Javier for a long time. Now that she had, she wasn't letting go easily.

"Consuela." I used an alpha voice. "Let go."

Her ears flicked.

A deep wrinkle appeared across the top of Javier's nose and his face flushed. He looked as if he might shoot us at any moment.

"Please, Consuela. *Por favor.*"

The dog released Javier's leg and grinned at me with blood-stained teeth.

If the man didn't shoot us both, he was going to feed us to the lions.

"We'll go now." I scooped up Consuela and ran out of the room before he could act on either plan.

# TWENTY-ONE

Where did I hide a list of account numbers and passwords that could get me killed? Javier knew I was up to something. If he had my room searched, they'd look in all the obvious places—between the mattress and box springs, under a corner of the carpet, in my lingerie drawer.

With the paper clenched in my hand, I wandered into the closet and found the answer.

Chances were excellent neither Javier nor his men knew about the secret compartments in Baker Street bags. I was fashion savvy and I hadn't known.

I lifted the amethyst clutch off the shelf and pushed and poked and turned until the compartment opened. The paper, rolled and folded, just fit.

I returned the bag to the shelf and put on one of the flowing day dresses Javier had provided. I loaded up an arm with Ippolita bracelets, put a two-carat diamond in each ear lobe, draped a gold necklace around my throat, and fastened the clasp. I even perused the array of sandals and found a pair that didn't hurt the still-healing skin on my feet.

Next—hair and make-up (I knew all Chariss's tricks and

used them). After a few minutes' consideration, I didn't cover the Z on my cheek.

If I wowed Ignacio Quintero with my beauty and charm, or if I gained his sympathy with my terrifying Zeta experience, the lions would have to find something else to eat. And, maybe—maybe—he'd let me go home.

As ready as I'd ever be, I sat down and waited with Consuela.

*Tap, tap.*

"Come in."

Manuel opened the door. "I'm here to escort you to lunch."

Lunch. There was no way I'd be able to eat a single bite. My stomach lurched at the thought. I set Consuela down on the floor, stood, and grabbed the chair for balance. I who had zero acting skills, was about to put on a life-altering performance.

*Stage fright* didn't cover the butterflies street-fighting in my stomach.

If I flubbed my lines, the consequences could be much worse than a bad review.

I peeled my fingers off the back of the chair, followed Manuel to the dining room, and paused in the doorway to steal a glance at Chariss's portrait.

Ignacio Quintero rose from his seat at the head of the table. "*Mi amiga*, I am honored to meet you."

Deer caught in headlights had more mobility than I did.

Ignacio Quintero, the most powerful Narco in the world, stepped out from behind his table, approached me, and brushed gentle kisses against each of my frozen cheeks.

*Yip. Yip, yip, yip.* Consuela demanded his attention.

He bent, picked her up, and cuddled her in his arms. "I am told you two are great friends."

"She is a very sweet dog." My face felt as if it might crack into a million pieces but at least my voice worked.

"Yes." He dropped a kiss on Consuela's head. "*Mi querida*." He reached out for my hand. "Come. Sit next to me."

Ignacio had thick, dark hair threaded with silver, brown eyes, and a strong chin. The arms that held Consuela were corded with muscle. His torso had thickened with middle age and wrinkles radiated from his eyes.

*He's old enough to be my father.*

What would I do if he joined me in my suite?

I didn't have an answer.

Ignacio let go of my hand and pulled out the chair next to his. "Please, sit."

I sat. And looked around the table.

There was Javier. He wore a simmering-rage expression and glared at Consuela.

And there was a man I didn't know seated across from me.

I'd met men like him before—pouty lips, cold eyes—spoiled sons of sultans, pampered princes of eastern realms. Men who prayed to Allah during the day and filled their luxury suites with high-end call girls at night. They had so much money there was nothing they couldn't buy. All that privilege and power corroded their souls.

"Abdul, may I present Poppy Fields." Ignacio tilted his chin my direction. "*Mi amiga*, this is Abdul Kabir."

So the plan to import Afghani heroin proceeded.

"Pleased to meet you." Thank God my voice still worked because the smile I wore was as brittle and breakable as old twigs.

"Likewise." Abdul Kabir's glance said he had my number —Hollywood slut. "Señor Quintero—"

"Ah, ah!" Señor Quintero wagged his finger.

"Ignacio—" Abdul corrected "—was kind enough to share a few of your mother's films with me as we traveled back here." No sarcasm. Not a hint.

The brittle smile remained in place. "I hope you enjoyed them."

"She is a beautiful woman. You look just like her."

"Thank you." No sarcasm. Not a hint.

Ignacio, with Consuela on his lap, beamed at his guests.

Abdul turned toward our host. "We have much to discuss."

"Later."

Abdul blinked. "But—"

"We will not talk business with a beautiful woman at the table."

Abdul's pout became more pronounced. "I am due in Venezuela tomorrow. When shall we talk business? Not on the plane while Chariss Carlton's films are playing. Not in the car where your driver might listen. Not now with your woman at the table."

If Abdul said something I shouldn't know, I'd never get out of here. I pushed my chair away from the table. "I am feeling a bit tired."

"Do not move." Ignacio grabbed my wrist and held fast. "Sit. You will eat with us." Then he turned his gaze on Abdul.

The Afghani man paled. And he didn't even know about the lions and their nutritional needs. "When? When will we discuss business?" Either the man was incredibly brave or incredibly stupid. Possibly both.

"Later."

Abdul sat straight in his chair. "I am not a Sinaloan peasant to be put off."

Consuela shot me a keep-your-mouth-closed-and-don't-move look.

Sound advice.

I didn't move. Not a muscle.

The little dog turned toward Abdul, pulled her lips back from her teeth until she resembled a vampire, and made a zombie sound deep in her throat.

Wisely, Abdul fell silent.

Thankfully, two men entered with our lunches—grilled fish, rice, and slaw plated on the first Señora Quintero's china.

They served us and left. Quickly.

We picked up heavy silver forks and poked at our meals. I poked. The men ate.

Ignacio shifted his attention to me—to my cheek. "The men who hurt you will pay, *mi amiga*."

I touched the scab and smiled bravely.

Javier snorted softly.

Ignacio shifted his attention again. "This happened on your watch." The glare he gave his CFO was enough to melt the paint from the walls.

I ventured a second brave smile. "Javier has been a most accommodating host in your absence."

*Yip.*

"This afternoon, I will show you around my home."

Abdul made a low sound in his throat. Not quite Consuela's zombie sound but close.

"You must see my horses. I raise Aztecas.

"She stole two."

*Yip.*

"The Zeta who took her stole two and if you'd been doing your job, that wouldn't have happened."

Javier remained defiantly unconvinced that a Zeta had abducted me. His lip curled.

"Who else would come for her but the Zetas?"

"How did they know she was here?"

"How would anyone know she was here?"

Javier didn't have an answer for that.

"Are the Zetas organized enough to plot against you?" Abdul's dark brows lowered. "You said they were but a shadow of what they had been."

"That is true."

"It better be. We've got a lot riding on this."

*Yip.*

I kept quiet, staring down at the fish I couldn't bring myself to eat.

"My word is good. We will have Nuevo Laredo within six months."

There. That was one of the things I shouldn't know. The butterflies in my stomach stopped their senseless fighting and tied knots. Lots and lots of knots. I put down my fork.

"You don't like your lunch?

"I'm not very hungry."

"We will fix you something else."

"It's not that. I'm—" I searched my plate for something to say "—I'm just nervous meeting you."

Javier made a gagging sound.

*Yip.*

"Miss Fields, how did you come to be in Mexico?" Abdul's expression was mocking. He had nothing but contempt for the woman who got herself kidnapped.

"I was invited to attend a resort opening."

Ignacio beamed proudly. "My latest property." He kissed the tips of his finger. "So beautiful."

Ignacio owned the resort? Had my kidnapping been planned? A scheme from the very beginning? Maybe. Probably. But Marta's death hadn't been part of the plan. The Zetas had colored outside the lines with that. "The resort is yours?"

"I own a majority interest. Abdul and his people own the rest."

Everything stilled. Everything. My heart. My blood. My vision. The men around me were frozen in time.

What better way to launder drug money than through resorts? The managers could overstate the number of rooms booked. And drinks served. And meals eaten. No one would look askance at a large amount of U.S. dollars—the tourists brought them.

Who did Brett Cannon work for? Ignacio or Abdul? Either

way, he worked for a criminal. Was he the one who'd alerted Javier I was headed to the airport? And what about Agent Gonzales who'd refused to return my passport? Was he in Ignacio's pocket?

The butterflies tied more knots.

*Yip.*

I found my voice. "This—" I waved my hand at the elegant dining room "—my coming here was planned before I set foot in Mexico?"

"I was delighted you accepted my invitation."

"Why me?" A stupid question. The answer was hanging on the wall wearing a red dress and a mantilla. I nodded toward Chariss's portrait. "I saw her on the news. She's worried sick."

A shadow crossed over Ignacio's face. "I'll make it up to her."

That shadow was nothing compared to the thunderstorm on Abdul's face. "You risked our investment for this *eahira*?

Given his tone, it was easy to guess what *eahira* meant.

Ignacio's hand slammed against the table. The silverware jumped. The water in the goblets jumped. I jumped. "No more talking."

We all studied our plates.

Somehow I managed a few bites of fish. Sawdust-flavored fish.

Lunch lasted another thirty interminable minutes.

At the end, I'd consumed three bites of fish and two bites of rice. Not a single bit of slaw.

Ignacio rose from his chair and extended his hand to me. "A quick tour, then I must attend to business."

Abdul scowled. Deeply.

Javier looked mildly amused.

I stood and took Ignacio's hand.

"This way." He led me through the house, past rooms I'd not yet seen. Past an ornate office. Past an arsenal. Past the kitchen where men ate at an enormous farmhouse table. They stood as we passed.

Outside, Ignacio tucked my hand into the crook of his arm and looked down at my shoes. "You're not dressed for the stable."

"No."

"Perhaps a short walk then I must deal with Abdul."

"A walk would be lovely. I haven't been outside since—" I touched my cheek.

"Javier was keeping you safe."

Javier was keeping an eye on me.

"Your home is beautiful."

"*Gracias.*"

We walked down a crushed gravel path that meant sure destruction for the Jimmy Choos covering my feet.

I wobbled.

Ignacio steadied me.

I smiled up at him with one of Chariss's smiles. "I think you are my mother's biggest fan."

"I am."

"Why Chariss?"

"She's the most beautiful woman in the world. And, what an actress. When her eyes fill with tears, I cry. When she laughs, I feel her joy. When she is angry, my fists clench with fury."

Who could argue with that?

"Here we are. My babies."

We stood in front of a fifteen-foot tall fence. On the other side, two lions lounged. The male regarded me with golden eyes then yawned. The female ignored me completely.

"Someday, I will have a private zoo. But for now, they are enough."

"That fence will hold them?" The lions were enormous. Their wildness barely contained by the bars that held them.

He gave me an indulgent smile. "The fence will hold them."

"They're gorgeous."

"As are you, my dear." He glanced at his watch and frowned. "I must deal with Abdul. What would you like to do this afternoon?"

"May I ride?" If there was a trail off this mountain, I'd find it.

"Yes, yes, whatever you wish." For an instant, the drug lord standing next to me looked almost shy. "I brought you a few gifts. They're in your room. I hope you will do me the honor of wearing them tonight. Dinner is at eight."

How could I say no?

# TWENTY-TWO

Planning my escape on horseback with four armed *sicarios* riding next to me proved impossible.

After a couple of hours, we rode back to the stables and I returned to my room.

Wrapped packages covered every inch of the bed.

I pulled the largest one toward me and slid my finger under the taped edge of the wrapping paper. Folding the paper back revealed a Valentino box. Valentino—Chariss's favorite designer.

A gown in the softest shade of lavender lay swaddled in tissue paper. I didn't dare touch the fabric—not with hands fresh from the stable.

I opened a smaller box. Inside lay a triple strand of enormous South Sea pearls held together with a diamond clasp. Other boxes held a matching bracelet and earrings. Ignacio was a generous gift giver.

I showered away the horse smell, did my hair and make-up, and put on the dress. It was too short. I'd have to wear flat sandals.

The pearls—being pearls—were just right.

I glanced at the Rolex watch Ignacio had provided. Still

thirty minutes till dinner. But, without Consuela, my room was lonely. And boring. When I tried the door to the hall, I found it unlocked. I slipped out into the hallway and walked toward the dining room.

Voices stopped me.

Loud voices.

Angry voices.

Unintelligible voices except for one word. *Venti.*

I backed away—quickly—turning on my heel and hurrying toward my bedroom as if pursued by a pack of killer Chihuahuas. Being bored and alone was better than getting caught eavesdropping.

I opened the door. "*Eeeek!*"

A sicario was on his hands and knees next to my bed. He regarded me with a slack jaw and wide eyes.

I pressed my hands against my chest. "What are you doing?" I demanded. I knew exactly what he was doing. He was here at Javier's behest. Searching my room.

The man gaped at me.

"Why are you here?" Outrage. I needed to sound outraged. "Why are you in my room?"

"Consuela lost her collar."

Seriously? That was the best he could come up with? He should have pretended not to understand English.

"I don't think it's in here." My smile said I believed his lie.

"I have to look."

"Sorry to disturb you. I forgot my lipstick." I hurried into the bathroom, grabbed a tube, then went into the closet and lifted the amethyst Baker Street bag off its shelf.

With the *sicario* watching, I dropped the lipstick into the bag. "Now I'm ready for dinner." Sounding carefree—that was the ticket. Not giving the man a hint as to my galloping nerves—that was the other ticket. "I hope you find her collar." I waved gaily and sashayed out the door with the weight of his stare draped across my shoulders like a mink stole.

Ignacio, wearing a suit to rival one of Javier's bespoke ensembles, met me in the hall. "I was on my way to escort you to dinner."

"How thoughtful."

"What's that?" He pointed to the bag in my hand.

"A handbag. It looks like a pretty rock doesn't it?" I opened the bag and handed it to him.

He glanced at my lipstick then returned the bag. "Nowhere near as lovely as you."

*Blech.* "You're too kind."

He tucked my hand into the crook of his arm. "Abdul will leave in the morning and then we'll have plenty of time together."

*Double blech.* I manufactured a smile.

Ignacio led me to the dining room where Abdul and Javier waited. Both men wore suits that probably cost as much as small cars. Neither looked happy to see me. Then again, they didn't look happy in general. Probably that Venti argument I'd overheard.

Ignacio pulled out my chair and waited while I sat.

When I was properly situated, he claimed his own chair at the head of the table.

Outside the light turned from lavender to violet.

Inside candles warmed the room with a soft glow.

Wine was poured—a Chilean red.

Ignacio lifted his glass. "*Salud!*"

Even Abdul drank.

"Tonight," said Ignacio. "I would like to hear stories of you and your mother."

Really? Give a girl a little warning. I searched my memory for something sweet, or uplifting, or even an example of Chariss being a decent parent. Nothing. But Ignacio loved Chariss. He wanted feel-good stories.

"Being an actress is hard work."

Ignacio nodded.

Javier stared out the French doors.

Abdul yawned.

"She always told me she wanted a better, more stable life for me."

Ignacio smiled as if entranced.

Javier glanced at his ridiculously expensive watch.

Abdul sneered at me and emptied the contents of his wine glass.

"She sent me to public high school." I was boring myself.

Ignacio leaned toward me.

Javier stood. "Please excuse me for a moment."

Abdul refilled his glass.

Outside, night was falling.

Inside, I was failing at recounting charming childhood memories of Chariss. "She was wonderful when I was asked to dances. We'd go shopping for dresses and jewelry." I touched the pearls at my neck and missed my father's locket. "There was one dance when we couldn't find the right dress and she called Karl Lagerfeld. He flew to L.A. and designed a dress especially for me."

Were the only good memories I had of Chariss linked to shopping?

Chariss had shared generously of her pocketbook and her make-up people and the stylist who could work miracles with my hair. What she hadn't shared was herself.

I blinked back a tear.

"You miss your lovely mother?" Ignacio patted my hand. "You will see her soon. I promise."

Abdul finished another glass of wine.

I glanced out at the night. I needed a better story. An actual story.

What was that? There were shadows. Running. I squinted. Something was happening outside.

*Tat-tat-tat-tat-tat-tat.*

A scream pierced the window.

Ignacio pushed away from the table, knocking his chair over. He spent half a second looking out the window then he disappeared through the nearest door.

I stood too. Which way was the room where I'd seen the guns? If Ignacio's hacienda was under attack by Zetas, I needed a weapon.

Something flared outside and I threw myself on the floor.

For an instant, the world was reduced to a deafening roar and flame. And weight. Heavy weight.

The table had collapsed on top of me.

I waited for the ringing in my ears to stop then crawled out from under the table's singed expanse.

Abdul hadn't been as lucky as me. His body was burned. Badly. He wasn't moving.

I stared at him for a moment. Frozen. Then the desire to stay alive kicked in.

I turned and tripped on the little bag I'd carried to dinner. It lay amongst the rubble, unscathed. I picked it up and ran.

Smoke. Smoke everywhere.

My eyes watered. I coughed. I ran to the place most likely to keep me breathing.

In Ignacio's arsenal, the weapons were untouched. I ignored the assault rifles (I'd never used one), grabbed a Glock and a magazine, and racked the slide. I stuffed a few extra magazines into the pockets of my dress. Now what?

There was no higher ground where I might defend myself.

I had no allies.

I had no transportation.

The sound of gunfire was constant.

I grabbed an assault rifle. How hard could it be to use?

I peeked out into the empty hallway and thought. Hard. If I could make it to the woods, I could hide until the battle was over.

I slipped into the hallway and, keeping my back pressed

against the wall, side-stepped away from the front of the house.

Voices.

I couldn't go that way.

My feet took me one of the few places they knew—the theater.

I leapt onto the stage and hid behind the curtain.

The voices grew louder. And I recognized one of them.

I peeked out from behind the curtain. Ignacio had his hands up and a man with an automatic rifle, similar to the one slung over my shoulder, looked as if he might shoot at any second.

"*Dónde está?*"

Ignacio shook his head. Either he didn't know the answer to the man's question or he was willing to die to keep a secret.

For all his talk of loving Chariss and being my friend, he'd left me in that dining room. Not the kind of man willing to die for a secret. My guess was he didn't know the answer.

What he did know was how to get out of the house and off the mountain.

Still hidden, I pointed the Glock at the man with the rifle. My hand slicked with sweat. My trigger finger shook. Shooting at a target was one thing. Shooting at a living, breathing human was something else entirely.

Noise erupted in the hallway and two more men burst into the theater. A man I'd never seen before pressed a gun against Manuel's head.

"*Dónde está?*" repeated the man with the rifle.

Ignacio held up his hands in surrender and shook his head. "*No sé.*"

"*Voy a disparar!*" The man holding Manuel had a face filled with rage—or maybe blood lust. Either way, it was terrifying.

Tears ran down Manuel's soot-stained face.

Ignacio shook his head.

The man holding Manuel shrugged and—

I stepped out from behind the curtain and pulled the trigger. I shot the man with the gun pressed to Manuel's head. Shot the man with the rifle. Shot too late.

Manuel fell to the floor with the dead Zetas.

Horror washed over me.

Ignacio stared at me for a moment then he held out his hand. "We have to get out of here."

But I couldn't move. The bodies on the floor of the theater —I'd done that. I'd killed them and I hadn't saved Manuel.

More gunfire erupted in the hall.

"We have to go!" Ignacio bent and pulled the blood slick rifle out of the dead man's hands. He straightened. "Now!"

Ignacio was my best chance for getting out of the house alive. I forced my feet forward and jumped off the stage. "How?"

"This way." He ran toward his Chariss room. A room with no windows and one door. A trap.

"Where are we going?"

"There's a tunnel."

Of course there was.

He opened the door and dashed inside.

Consuela stood in the middle of the room, growling.

Ignacio ignored her, grabbed the photo off the desk, and ran to the far wall. He pushed a photo of Chariss aside, pressed something, and a hidden door opened.

Without looking back at me or Consuela, he ran through it.

*Yip?*

The gunfire was louder. Closer.

*Tat-ta-tat-tat-tat-tat.*

"Let's go."

Consuela didn't move.

I scooped her up, ran through the door, and stopped. I couldn't leave the door open. The Zetas would follow. I leaned my shoulder against its weight and pushed.

*Click.*

I took a breath and looked around.

I stood in a dimly lit vestibule the size of a coat closet. A set of stairs descended into the darkness.

*Tat-tat-tat-tat-tat-tat.*

I took another breath—one that tasted like death—and inched my way down the stairs.

At the bottom, the tunnel turned at a right angle. The light was dim but the air smelled fresh.

Above me someone pounded on the door.

Friend or foe?

*Tat-ta-tat-tat-tat-tat.*

I ran.

And ran. My lungs burned. The tunnel felt endless. With each step, a rifle banged against one hip, a handbag with sharp edges banged against the other, and the dog in my arms wriggled wildly.

I stopped and put Consuela down. "Keep up."

*Yip.* She ran ahead of me.

I followed her.

The little dog ran faster than I did. Then again, she hadn't been nearly blown up or killed someone. I stumbled.

I'd killed two someones.

And I couldn't think about that now.

Nor could I think about Manuel staring sightlessly at the theater's starry ceiling.

I ran. I ran with a stitch in my side and the certainty that the assault rifle and my hip were not friends. Maybe even enemies. At least the tunnel sloped downward. I ran until the rasp of my breath and the click of Consuela's nails on the hard-packed earth were the only sounds.

Consuela was tiny, but she was also fast—with a quick darting speed that left me behind. There were moments when I couldn't hear her at all.

*Yip. Yip, yip, yip.*

I rounded a bend. The tunnel ended and Consuela waited at the mouth of a yawning hole. We stood at the top of vertigo-inducing steps.

I picked her up, arranged the rifle and handbag, and eased my foot onto the first step.

Descending the steps in the dark wasn't easy. Drops of perspiration trickled from my hairline to my chin.

Consuela shifted in my arm.

"Be still."

How had my life come to this? Alone in the dark inside a Sinaloan mountain? I sniffed.

*Yip.*

"I'm not feeling sorry for myself." I totally was.

*Yip.* Consuela wasn't fooled.

If my father found himself in a Sinaloan mountain, he'd have planned his next move. He wouldn't have wasted a second questioning the choices that brought him there.

I straightened my spine against the pull of the rifle, took a deep breath, and found the next step.

Down, down, down. Finally, my lower foot found earth and the space around me opened up. Light seeped around a corner.

I put Consuela down and she ran toward the light.

I followed her.

The tunnel widened and the light grew brighter. The air freshened.

Another turn. And another.

Consuela waited for me at a corner. I stopped and peeked around.

I blinked against the brightness then narrowed my eyes. There was Ignacio. He stood in what looked like a garage—poured cement floor, a door big enough for a vehicle, and a couple of ATVs.

He pushed a button and the door rose, welcoming a whoosh of night air.

Consuela ran to him.

Ignacio grinned, scooped the dog into his arms, then looked back toward the corner where I hid.

"*Estás aquí.*"

Ignacio's head whipped around and I couldn't see his expression. Was he as surprised to see Javier as I was?

Javier, who'd stared out the window and checked his watch then disappeared a moment before the attack. Javier, who pointed a gun at Ignacio. Javier, whose lips curled in a sneer.

Rapid Spanish ensued.

If, by some miracle, I got off this mountain, I would learn Spanish.

I might not have understood their words, but their meaning was clear. Only one of the men would be walking out of the garage. If it was Javier, and he found me, I'd be as dead as Ignacio.

I backed into the shadows of the tunnel.

Just in time.

A volley of gunfire exploded, near deafening in the tunnel.

Then silence.

My limbs shook and sweat plastered my dress to my skin. Who was alive? Who was dead?

Then came the sound of a motor turning. One of the ATVs roared to life, its engine reverberating through the tunnel.

After a moment, the noise faded.

I was alone.

I gathered my courage, tightened my grip on the Glock, and crept toward the exit.

## TWENTY-THREE

Consuela sat close to Ignacio's body. Her head hung low and her ears drooped.

I'd hoped—sincerely hoped—that Ignacio had prevailed.

"Consuela, come."

The little dog looked at me and stayed where she was.

Tears welled in my eyes. Not for Ignacio—he didn't deserve my tears. I cried for the dog who'd loved him.

She could stay with him until I was ready to leave.

Javier had roared off on an ATV. Presumably Javier knew how to ride one, was familiar with the terrain, and was not worried about turning on a headlight. None of those things were true for me.

I couldn't ride down the mountain on one of those things. Nor could I stay where I was—eventually, someone was going to realize my body wasn't under the dining room table.

I looked around. Besides the ATVs, there wasn't much—a case of bottled water, parkas hung on hooks, a few backpacks, and a box of protein bars.

I put down the assault rifle, donned a parka, and filled a backpack with water, a couple of protein bars, and the Baker Street bag. Then I slung the rifle over my shoulder, shifted the magazines to the coat's pockets, opened a bottle of water, and took a long gulp.

"Consuela, we need to go."

She didn't move.

I bent and reached for her.

She snarled at me and snapped her teeth.

I snatched my hands away. "We can't stay here."

*Grrrrr.*

"If Javier finds you, he'll feed you to the lions."

Consuela merely blinked.

It felt wrong leaving her—like I was leaving my only friend—but staying was suicidal. I needed to get down the mountain. Find a town. Find a phone.

"I'm going." I walked toward the open air.

Outside, stars blazed in an obsidian sky. I looked back. The little dog was nestled against the dead man.

"Last chance." My voice was thick.

Consuela didn't move a muscle.

My throat closed and I walked alone into the night.

There was a trail. A trail that presumably led to a road. And the road presumably led to a town. I headed down the mountain.

In the distance, the occasional burst of gunfire interrupted the breeze whistling through the trees and the hoot of a hunting owl.

I walked, glad I'd donned flat shoes instead of heels—not that I didn't wish for thicker soles, ankle support, and closed toes. The path was rough and I felt the edge of every rock and wobbled on every root.

The feeling came slowly.

First, a hint—a mere goosebump.

Then an actual hint.

*Snap.*

Someone or something was watching me.

I gripped the Glock and kept a steady pace, afraid to look

over my shoulder.

The sound had come from behind me and to the left.

There was definitely something out there. The skin on the back of my neck crawled.

Around me there were trees and bushes and the sliver of a trail. No place I could defend. No place to hide and hope.

I tripped on the unraveling hem of the dress and steadied myself against a tree trunk. Apparently couture gowns weren't made for late night hikes through the woods.

*Snap.*

Now the sound was to my right.

My heart rose to my throat and I swallowed it back into place.

Ahead, the trail cut to the left. Where it turned, a large tree stood sentry.

If men were following me, plastering my back against that tree might be a death sentence. If the thing that went *snap* in the night was an animal, the tree might save my life.

The tree was ten feet away. I had to decide.

Man or beast?

Beast. It had to be a beast.

I took the last few steps to the tree, pushed against its broad expanse, and lifted the Glock.

Blood beat in my ears and I used one hand to steady the other.

"Who's there?"

Silence.

I peered into the night and my heart stopped.

Even in the darkness, I could see their eyes glinting. There were two of them. Lions. And they thought I was a late-night snack.

I'd already killed two people and now I had to kill lions? Seriously?

The sad truth was I'd probably feel worse about killing the lions.

What now? Could I scare them away?

One was to my left, the other to my right.

I took aim and shot a tree between them.

The male lion, the one on the left, roared.

Great. I'd made him mad.

What now?

The female, the one on the right, crept toward me. I shot at her paws.

Now she roared.

I should pull the trigger—shoot them.

But I couldn't.

The male lion slunk forward.

Surviving meant doing things I couldn't do.

I raised the gun.

*Yip.*

Consuela appeared and took a combative stance between me and the giant cats—as if she believed she was a Rhodesian Ridgeback and not a Chihuahua.

The lions blinked.

The little dog growled.

"Consuela, no." She'd be an *amuse bouche* before their main meal. Me.

She danced on her paws—they'd have to catch her first.

Another roar, in the distance.

Another lion? How lucky could one girl get?

Except the roar was steady and growing louder.

A helicopter.

A searchlight cut through the trees. Blinding me. Blinding the lions. Blinding Consuela.

*Yip! Yip, yip, yip!*

The female lion inched closer. Close enough for starlight to gleam on her teeth.

Shooting her felt like a terrible crime but I raised the gun—

A bright light hit me right in the eyes.

I pulled the trigger. And missed.

Was the helicopter pilot *trying* to get me killed?

At least the lioness retreated.

The light swung from me to the cats. They liked the glare even less than I did.

With a roar of displeasure, the male lion melted into the trees. With a lick of her lips that promised she'd be back, the female followed him.

My back slid down the tree's trunk—mainly because all the strength in my knees had disappeared with the lions.

Consuela ran to me, nudged me, reminded me with a nip that staying still meant death. The helicopter and its lights would return any second now.

I pushed myself off the ground. "I'm glad you're here." I told her. "You were very brave."

She preened. *Yip.*

I stepped onto the trail and a scream split the night. A man's scream. A shock and terror and agony scream. A scream that sent shivers skittering down my spine and raised the hackles on Consuela's back.

"I think the lions found dinner," I whispered.

An unfortunate man had just died an unthinkable death. Probably a *sicario*. And since *sicarios* seldom traveled alone, there were probably others out there—one or two or ten. Were they looking for me? Were they Zetas or Sinaloans? And now that Ignacio was dead, did that matter?

My steps were long and fast and purposeful—get down the mountain, find a phone, call for help. I ignored the pain in my feet, the weakness in my knees, and the deep-rooted desire to curl up in a little ball. Consuela trotted to keep up with me.

There! The road—such as it was. I could have called it a pair of dirt ruts leading to Ignacio's hacienda. Better yet, a pair of ruts leading away from Ignacio's hacienda.

I dared not walk in those ruts—a truck could overtake me

in seconds. Instead, I used the ruts as a guide. I tripped through the woods, falling often. Bushes grabbed at the fabric of my skirt. Sticks and stones tried to break my frigid, bare toes. The backpack and rifle weighed more with each step. And the Glock in my hand felt heavy—almost too heavy to lift.

But the worst was the helicopter. It passed overhead every few minutes, its light freezing me beneath the overhang of branches. I couldn't help but think it was looking for me. Had Javier guessed that I'd stolen Ignacio's account numbers? Was he searching for me? Or, was it Jake?

And what of the *sicarios* the lions hadn't killed? Were they searching the woods? Looking for me?

Get down the mountain, find a phone, call for help. I repeated those words like a litany.

Get down the mou—I froze. The helicopter was back.

A voice crackled over the helo's loudspeaker. Jake's voice. "There's a poppy field a klick down the road."

If the *sicarios* were looking for me, they'd know where to find me. Or maybe they wouldn't. Maybe they'd think the DEA was going after one of their poppy fields. Either way, that klick down the road promised peril and my best chance of getting out of Sinaloa alive.

I leaned against the nearest tree and thought. Jake knew the mountain was lousy with killers. Had he really meant to send them all to one spot? And me too?

I rested my face in my hands.

Unless there was a platoon on that helicopter, we could all be killed.

What choice did I have?

Consuela yipped softly and I raised my head. There were men on the road. At least a dozen. Men with automatic rifles, fierce expressions, and bloodied hands. I stepped farther back into the shadows and held my breath.

They streamed past me. Zetas? Sinaloans? They wore

plaid shirts. Did Zetas wear plaid? Or, was plaid a strictly Sinaloan fashion statement?

When the last man had disappeared, I ventured out of the trees.

Twelve men had passed me. All with automatic rifles. The smell of death trailed after them. And Jake wanted me to follow them.

I looked at Consuela.

She looked at me.

We both shrugged and began walking.

Another turn. The side of the road rose but the road did not. If I followed my current path, I'd be above the road. The other choice was one of the ruts—easier walking but more dangerous in every way that counted.

I climbed, my thighs burning, my ruined dress twisting around my ankles like a snare.

Up. And up.

*Yip.* Consuela's tongue hung out of the side of her mouth.

"We're almost to the top."

Below us the road snaked through the darkness.

Above us the stars shined like beacons.

We climbed.

At the crest, we stopped. I slid the gun and backpack off my shoulders, opened a bottle of water, drank deeply, then cupped my hand and poured water for Consuela.

She drank from my palm, her little pink tongue lapping thirstily.

When she'd had her fill, I stood (my knees and back and hips objected) and walked to the edge of the ridge, searching for a break in the trees, a place where Jake and his team might land a helicopter.

The night gave up no secrets.

"At least going down will be easier."

Consuela did not look convinced. Not then. Not when I put on the backpack. Not when I picked up the rifle.

I took four steps on the down slope. Four steps until a rock shot out from under my foot. Four steps until I landed on my hiney. Four steps until I slid down the side of a mountain on a hiney covered only by a silk dress and La Perla panties. Four steps until the rifle was ripped off my shoulder by a sapling.

A herd of elephants would have been stealthier.

I sat at the bottom, covered in pine needles, cuts, abrasions, and dirt. The couture dress wasn't fit for use as a rag.

*Yip?*

"I'm okay," I lied.

I pushed off the ground (it was getting more difficult each time I did it) and rolled my neck. At least I still had the Glock and the backpack.

I stood and listened, dreading the footsteps that surely must be coming. People in Mazatlan had probably heard me descend that ridge.

I heard nothing. "Let's go." We had a rendezvous at a poppy field.

# TWENTY-FOUR

I limped through the thinning woods. One of the straps on my sandal had broken during my fall and keeping the shoe on my foot was a trial. I bent, adjusted the shoe for the three-hundred-seventeenth time, and caught a movement out of the corner of my eye.

A *sicario* crept through the trees to my right.

I held my breath and prayed he wouldn't hear the hammering of my heart.

He passed me, edged his way to the place where the trees ended, and dropped to one knee with the stock of his rifle planted in his shoulder.

He was there to shoot Jake.

There were moments when I wanted to shoot Jake. Lots of them. This moment was not one of them. Jake and his helicopter represented my best chance of getting out of Sinaloa alive.

I scanned the woods.

Twelve men had walked past me. Where were the other eleven?

Above us, the helicopter circled, the whir of its engines and rotors loud enough to drown out all other sounds.

The *sicario's* gaze was fixed on the field.

My gaze was fixed on the *sicario*. I stood. Slowly.

An arm wrapped around my neck, tightening into a head lock. The scents of tobacco and sweat and blood filled my nose.

For an instant, panic froze my limbs. Then ten years' worth of martial arts classes took over. I dropped my left knee to the ground.

The man who'd grabbed me rolled over my back.

*Crack.*

He thudded against the uneven earth.

I drew a ragged breath and pointed my Glock at his heart.

He just stared at me.

And stared.

And didn't move.

I dared a quick glance at Consuela. "You could have warned me."

She looked at me with an I-tried-but-the-helicopter-was-too-loud-and-you-weren't-paying-attention expression on her face.

I returned my gaze to the man on the ground. He still hadn't moved, still hadn't reacted at all.

I shifted my weight away from him.

Had I knocked him out? No. His eyes were open.

He hadn't even blinked. Not once.

I tapped his cheek (slapped his cheek).

Nothing.

I sat back on my heels and stared at his sightless eyes.

My hand covered my mouth and the moan rising from deep in my soul. I'd killed him. And not just him. My tally for the night stood at three. Three men who wouldn't return to their wives or children because of me.

I wrapped my arms around my waist and rocked back and forward.

Consuela rubbed her head against my thigh. *Yip.* A pull-yourself-together yip.

But I couldn't. With shaking fingers, I reached behind the man's head and found a rock. A wet rock. I yanked my fingers away but it was too late. His blood, warm and horrifying, was literally on my hands.

I wiped my hand on my ruined dress and choked on a sob.

*Yip.* Consuela regarded me with narrowed eyes. She had no patience for guilt. Not when there were still eleven *sicarios* lurking in the darkness.

I glanced at the *sicario* at the edge of the woods. He hadn't moved. Hadn't heard a thing. The helicopter's roar had hidden the sounds of his comrade's death.

That roar grew louder as the helicopter descended, close enough to whip my hair around my face. Close enough to blow Consuela's lips away from her gums.

The *sicario* stared down the barrel of his rifle.

When the helicopter landed, he'd shoot at the people who'd come to rescue me.

Dammit.

I gripped the Glock and snuck toward him. My heart, in its attempts to jackhammer its way out of my chest, was louder than the helicopter. My mouth was so dry my tongue stuck to the roof of my mouth. My hands shook.

Closer.

Closer, until I stood behind him.

I screwed up my face (and my courage), lifted my arms high, and brought the Glock down on the back of his head.

He collapsed onto a pile of dead leaves. Dead or unconscious?

Please, please, unconscious.

I didn't check. I couldn't bear another death. I just bent, picked up his rifle, and backed into the cover of the trees.

In the field, the helicopter's landing skids were just feet from the ground.

The skids touched and men wearing body armor leapt from the cargo area, crouching as they hit the ground.

The first shots came from my left, explosions of white light and deafening sound.

The men in the field dropped to their bellies and returned fire.

I dropped to my belly because my knees gave way.

Consuela huddled next to me and I pulled her close.

Deafening. So many guns. So many bullets. The woods were on fire with flashes. How could anyone get through this alive?

There was no way I was walking away from this. We were all going to die, ripped apart by indiscriminate bullets.

There were so many things I'd wanted to do—publish a book, fix my relationship with Chariss, make a difference. Dying in Sinaloan woods, caught between DEA agents and *sicarios*, was never part of the plan.

Gradually, the barrage slowed.

When the guns finally stopped, the silence was loud—a whiteness pressing against my ears.

One by one, the men in the field stood. Body armor and training had prevailed.

I pushed myself to my hands and knees and stood. Slowly.

*Yip.* Consuela looked up at me with wild eyes.

I stuffed the Glock into my coat pocket, bent and gathered the little dog into my arms.

The two of us staggered into the field.

"Halt!"

I halted.

"Put your hands up!"

With Consuela in my arms, I couldn't. I simply stopped walking.

"Poppy?" The voice belonged to Jake. "Poppy is that you?"

Who else? "It's me." My voice was raw.

Three men approached with their guns drawn.

I didn't move a muscle.

"Poppy?" Jake lowered his gun. "What happened to you?"

I stiffened. "I had a rough night." Maybe I didn't look my best. I'd nearly been incinerated, faced down lions, killed three (maybe four) men, slid down a mountain on my backside, and crawled through the woods. There wasn't a woman in the world who'd look fabulous after all that (except Chariss).

Jake stared for an eternity, his mouth hanging open. He shifted his gaze to the dog in my arms. "What is that?"

Consuela growled.

"This is Consuela. She's coming with me."

He was smart enough not to argue.

"Can we go? Please?"

"Yeah." He shook his head as if he'd just remembered we were standing in a poppy field surrounded by dead *sicarios*. "Let's get you to the helicopter." He reached his hand toward my elbow and Consuela's growl deepened.

"It's okay," I crooned. "He's a frien—he's here to help."

Consuela wasn't convinced. Her lips drew back from her bared teeth and her eyes narrowed.

Jake ignored the four-pound threat in my arms. "Do you need this?" He pulled at one of the backpack's straps.

"Yes!"

His brows rose but he left the backpack in place.

Instead, his arm circled my waist and he helped me limp to the helicopter.

A man in body armor pulled me inside. "Let's get you strapped in, miss."

Then he pulled at my backpack.

"I need my purse."

"What?"

"In the backpack, there's a purse. I need it."

He opened the pack and looked inside. "No purse in here, miss."

"It looks like an amethyst."

"A what?"

"A purple rock."

He dug around inside the pack then handed me the Baker Street bag. With the bag clutched in one hand and Consuela nestled in my other arm, I allowed Jake to tuck a blanket around my legs and buckle me into a seat.

Someone else clamped headphones onto my ears.

With a whir of rotors, the helicopter took off.

I awakened in a hospital room. Sterile. White. Scratchy sheets. The beep of a monitor. And the blessed sound of American voices outside the door.

The door opened and Jake stepped into the room. "You're awake."

"Where am I?" Every inch of my body hurt. Even my hair. And the effort it took to keep my eyes open was ridiculous.

"A hospital."

I lifted my head and glared at him. "What country?"

"The United States."

I let my head fall back on the pillow. "Where's Consuela?"

"She's in a kennel."

"She won't like that."

"No kidding." He held up a bandaged hand.

"You didn't hurt her?" My voice wavered.

"Of course not. The little dervish is fine."

Thank God. "Where's my purse?"

"Right there." He pointed.

I turned my head. The Baker Street bag sat glinting in the sunlight on the window sill.

"That must be quite a lipstick."

"What?"

"To drag that bag through the mountains, I mean."

"It's not the lipstick. It's the bag. Would you please bring it to me?"

Jake handed me the little bag.

I pushed and prodded and turned until the hidden compartment opened. The scrap of paper fell into my hand. "Here." I held it out to him.

"What's that?"

"A list of Ignacio Quintero's bank accounts with passwords."

"What!" He snatched the bit of paper from my fingers. "How did you get this?"

"It's a long story." And I was so, so tired. "Can I tell you later?"

"Of course."

"Can Consuela be in here with me? Please?"

My eyelids weighed too much. They fluttered closed before he answered.

When I opened my eyes again, the light had changed.

"Miss Fields."

I shifted my head and looked at the man sitting in the visitor's chair. Middle-aged, non-descript, thinning hair—totally forgettable except for the intelligence gleaming in his eyes. "Who are you?"

"My name is John Brown."

"Wow."

"Not as colorful a name as Poppy Fields."

"Few are."

He nodded, ceding my point. "You've had quite an adventure."

An adventure? The faces of the men I'd killed swam through my brain.

"Tell me about it." Ugh. I didn't want to talk about any of it. Least of all the dead men. "Who are you, Mr. Brown?"

"Jake works for me."

"You had him fake his death?"

He crossed his legs and leaned back in his chair. "That is a complicated question."

"No, it's not. There are only two possible answers."

"Then the answer is yes."

I turned my head away.

"We had reason to believe that the Jalisco Cartel was closing in on him. He was safer dead."

I had no answer for that.

"You spent time at Ignacio Quintero's hacienda."

"Yes." My throat was dry. "I need water."

John Brown handed me a blue plastic cup with a bendy straw.

I drank deeply.

"What did you observe?"

I returned the empty cup to him. "I need some more."

The skin around his eyes tightened but he picked up a pitcher, refilled the cup, and returned it to me.

"Thank you."

"About the hacienda—"

"I spent more time with Javier Diaz than I did with Ignacio."

John Brown resumed his seat, leaning forward in the chair and resting his elbows on his knees.

"Diaz acted like a CFO. I don't think he approved of Ignacio's plan to go into business with the Afghanis."

"Which Afghanis?"

"The only one there was Abdul Kabir."

A light flamed in John Brown's eyes.

"You talked to him?"

"Yes."

"What did he say?"

"Not much that I could understand. Anything important, they spoke Spanish and I don't speak much Spanish." I glanced around the hospital room. "Can you bring me the dog?"

Something like annoyance flashed across John Brown's face. The fate of a little dog wasn't terribly important to him. "Soon."

"Now."

Definitely annoyance.

"Maybe when we're done talking."

When I'd told him everything and had no leverage.

"Now would be better."

We stared at each other. We could stare till next Thursday. I wasn't saying another word until Consuela was in my arms.

The moment stretched.

And stretched.

John Brown stood, crossed the room to the door, and stuck his head into the hallway. "Miss Fields wants the dog."

Someone said something—too low for me to hear.

"I don't care. Get her the dog."

John Brown resumed his seat. "The dog will be here in a minute."

"I'll just wait till she arrives."

"Miss Fields, it seems as if you don't trust me."

"You work with Mérida."

He simply looked at me. Not confirming. Not denying.

"You had the power to return my passport, to get me out of Mexico, and you didn't."

"The situation was complicated."

"I think it's pretty simple. You deliberately put a U.S. citizen at risk."

"I'm sorry you see it that way."

"Is there another way to see it?"

The door pushed open and a pale-faced man in a tan suit carried a small crate into my room. Inside an animal snarled. He put the crate down on the edge of my bed and backed away.

"Consuela." I opened the crate's gate and the little dog burst out, spinning and baring her teeth at the men in the room. "Consuela." I held open my arms.

She looked back at me, obviously torn between coming to me or ripping out the men's throats.

I pursed my lips and made a kissing sound.

With a curl of her lip that promised eternal pain to those who crossed her, Consuela leapt into my arms and licked my chin.

I dropped a kiss on her little head. "Hello, brave girl."

John Brown cleared his throat.

"Abdul Kabir was there to negotiate moving Afghani heroin through Mexico. The Sinaloans planned on taking over Nuevo Laredo. My sense was that Javier was against the deal."

"Why?"

"I think he's responsible for the attack on the hacienda. I know he killed Ignacio."

The man in the chair rubbed his chin. "How do you know?"

"I was around the corner when he pulled the trigger." I stroked Consuela's fur.

John Brown rubbed his chin. "You're sure about that?"

"Yes."

"So Javier Diaz has taken over the Sinaloan Cartel." He leaned back. "What else?"

"What else do you want to know?"

"You tell me."

"I think Venti was Javier's pet project. I'm guessing he saw the Sinaloans with an exclusive distributorship for the hottest club drug around and thought there was more money there than in diluting the production stream for heroin with Afghani product."

"Oh?" John Brown's left eyebrow lifted and he tilted his chin. An indulgent smile played across his mouth. Clearly the man didn't agree with my assessment. "That's not what our intelligence suggests. Any proof of that?"

"No. None." But I knew it was true. I looked down at Consuela, who was snuggled in my arms.

"How did you get those account numbers?"

I looked up. "I found them in Ignacio's private office and copied them down."

"We've seized more than two hundred million dollars. Your country owes you a great debt, Miss Fields. What can we do to thank you?"

"I'd like to go home."

# TWENTY-FIVE

If my disappearance made international news, my safe return broke the internet. That I'd been kidnapped by Ignacio Quintero, that I'd escaped during an assault on his hacienda wearing torn couture and a small fortune's worth of pearls (which the DEA seized), that I'd fallen into James Ballester's waiting arms with a full phalanx of photographers snapping like mad—people couldn't get enough.

Except for me. I'd had more than enough.

Eclipsing Chariss, even for a few days, wasn't remotely fun.

I retreated to my house, hired a security service to keep the paparazzi at bay, and stared at the ocean.

Mia arrived with a weekend bag, a case of wine, and a box of dog biscuits. She slipped through the mob outside my front door and stared at the ocean with me.

Then a Kardashian announced her pregnancy and the photographers moved on. Consuela, Mia, and I were able to sit outside on the deck and stare at the ocean without worrying about photographers.

"Walk me through it again." Mia took a sip of her Sauvignon Blanc.

"Ignacio invited me to the resort to kidnap me."

"While he was on the other side of the world?"

"I think the kidnapping was planned for later in the week. Quintero was supposed to be back from the Middle East before I was taken. But, when things went wrong at the resort —when I decided to leave—Javier put his plan in motion." He'd made my abduction so public, left a dead Sinaloan on the toll road, and left a witness alive—it was guaranteed to be the lead story. Everywhere. "I think he wanted the Zetas blamed."

"I get that. But, why?"

"Javier wanted—wants—Nuevo Laredo. Anything that damages the Zetas is good."

Mia turned her face away from the ocean. "Why did Ignacio want you kidnapped in the first place?"

"In his mind it was a means of forming a bond with Chariss."

"Did he—"

"No. He never touched me."

She put her feet up on an ottoman and stared out at the waves from behind an oversized pair of Gucci sunglasses. "What about Marta?"

"I'm pretty sure the Zetas forced her to steal that information. But she didn't want to betray Javier. When she didn't turn over the flash drive to the Zetas, they killed her."

Consuela opened one eye, stared at me for a second, then drifted back to sleep.

"Anyone seeing pictures of Marta and me at that opening night party would have thought we were best friends. Since I was the last person to see her alive, the Zetas assumed I had the drive."

Mia sat up straighter. "That reminds me, I brought you Marta's purse. I think you should have it." She pushed out of her chair.

"Really, I don't want it." I wanted no reminders—not of

Marta or Ignacio or the men I'd killed. "I want nothing from that trip."

Mia's gaze shifted to Consuela and her eyebrows lifted above the rim of her glasses.

"Consuela's different. She took on two lions for me."

"Still, I think you should have that bag." She opened the door into the house. "I'm going to grab it for you now."

I didn't have the energy to argue. The handbag would end up on a shelf at the back of my closet. I would never carry it. Too many awful memories.

Consuela watched Mia leave, stood, stretched, and yipped at a seagull she judged to be too close to the deck.

A moment later, Mia, a glass of wine in one hand, the purse in the other, hurried back through the door.

Consuela, with a devilish expression on her little face, ran between Mia's legs.

Mia's arms cartwheeled. And her face reflected her dilemma. Drop the wine or drop the bag?

Mia never dropped wine. Ever.

The bag fell to the deck and skittered toward my feet.

With her free hand, Mia grabbed onto the back of a chair, and scowled at Consuela.

Consuela snickered.

I picked up the bag. "What's this?" A section of the bag had swung loose revealing a flash drive. "Did you hide something?"

"No." Mia shifted her scowl from Consuela to the bag in my lap. "There must be a second compartment."

I showed her the flash drive in my palm.

"I wonder what's on it."

"One way to find out." I swung my feet off the ottoman and went inside to the laptop on the kitchen counter.

Consuela and Mia followed me.

"Are you sure this is a good idea?" Mia took an extra big

sip of wine. "Looking at the last drive didn't turn out so well."

*Yip.*

"It'll be fine." Hopefully. I plugged in the drive and the file opened.

Words in Spanish. "Where's André when we need him?"

André had hugged me like he'd never let go, scolded me for getting kidnapped, told me he loved me, and hopped on a plane for France to meet a European sports agent who could help him make a gazillion euro.

I copied the text, pasted it into Google translate, and read.

Mia read over my shoulder. "That Venti is nasty stuff."

Very nasty stuff.

We read to the end then I closed the window.

"What's that?" she pointed to the open zip folder.

"I'll look." I opened an excel sheet. "Whoa."

"Whoa?"

"They're projecting sales to outpace Molly in a matter of months."

"You can read that?"

"I was an economics major, remember?"

"Yeah. But I didn't know you paid attention. I thought you took those classes to upset Chariss."

"I paid attention." Chariss had wanted a creative daughter. An artist. She'd been appalled when I declared as an economics major. I'd quietly taken every English and creative writing class I could and never told her about any of them.

"What are you going to do with this information?" Mia asked.

"Turn it over to the authorities as soon as possible." Another conversation with the sharp-eyed John Brown—this time I could prove I was right about Javier and Venti.

Mia stared out the window at the waves lapping against the beach and her lips thinned. "You're different. Since you came back, I mean."

I'd grown up. "I know."

"Have you heard from Jake?" Her voice was soft, almost gentle.

"No. Why?"

"We've talked about everything—the resort and Marta and Javier Diaz and Ignacio Quintero. We've talked about your failed escape and your actual escape. We've talked about everything but him."

First off, we hadn't talked about everything. I'd skipped the parts of the story where I killed people. Secondly, I didn't have anything to say about Jake. After our brief conversation in the hospital, he'd disappeared. Another wound. "I don't know where he is."

Mia's expression softened till it was perilously close to pity. "You need to go out. Party. Have fun."

Maybe the girl who'd gone to Mexico believed she could party her troubles away. The woman who'd come back knew a club, a cocktail, and a flirtation wouldn't solve a thing. "Not tonight."

*Bzzzzz.* My phone vibrated in my pocket.

I pulled it out and looked at the screen.

"What's wrong?"

"How do you know something is wrong?"

"You're pale."

"Chariss is here. She wants to talk."

"Do you want me to stay with you?"

Having a buffer was oh-so tempting but I shook my head. "I have to talk to her sometime. I might as well get it over with."

Mia gave me a quick hug. "I'll be on the deck if you need me."

I picked up Consuela, snuggled her close, and walked to the foyer.

My fingers curled around the door handle, I took a deep breath, and opened the front door.

Chariss blew in like a sirocco. She took one look at Consuela in my arms and curled her lip. "I can't believe you still have that dog."

"I'm keeping her."

"A drug lord's dog?"

"It's not the dog's fault. Besides, she's my dog now."

"Do you have any sparkling water?" If Chariss couldn't win an argument, she changed the subject. "I'm parched."

"Lime or grapefruit?"

"Plain."

"Sorry. No."

She favored me with a put-upon sigh. "Lime."

I put Consuela down, went to the bar, and fixed two drinks.

When I turned around, Chariss and Consuela were eying each other with obvious dislike. Both had their lips curled. Both showed a hint of teeth.

Chariss should be careful. Consuela might actually bite.

"Here." I handed her a glass.

Chariss perched on the edge of a sofa with her ankles crossed and her back straight. "You're mad at me."

I flopped into a chair. "I'm not."

"You blame me."

"I don't."

"That man kidnapped you because he was obsessed with me."

"That's not your fault."

Her mouth tightened. "But you still blame me."

"This isn't about you."

She blinked. "Then what is it about? What's making you so cold?"

"I killed people." The words slipped out—unbidden and unexpected. Why could I tell my mother what I'd done but not my best friend?

Chariss's jaw hinged open and her eyes widened. She'd

obviously planned this conversation, but I wasn't cooperating. I'd gone off script. "I'm sure they were bad people."

"They were still people."

"Bad people. I think you should come to Paris with me."

I blinked. We were done talking about my killing people? Already? "Paris?"

"You love Paris."

I did love Paris.

"I have to go back. Tomorrow. Come with me. You could disappear in Paris. Get away from the photographers. Hole up in a café on the Left Bank and write." She paused, took a small sip of her water, and a moue of distaste flitted across her lips. "When were you going to tell me you wrote a book?"

Not congratulations, or wow, or who knew you had any talent. "I don't know."

"Why didn't you tell me?"

"I wanted to accomplish something on my own. I didn't want it to be about you."

"So it's not about me?"

"The book? Or my decisions?"

"The book."

I stared as she smoothed the fabric of her dress then smoothed her forehead. "You thought I threw you under a literary bus?"

She didn't deny it.

The book. Barclift had promised me he could triple the advance if I published under Poppy Fields instead of Polly Feld. I'd declined. "That's what this invitation to Paris is about? The book?"

"No! I want you to come with me. We could spend time together. Go shopping."

In the woods, sure I was going to die, I'd regretted that Chariss's and my relationship was so strained. Now was my chance to fix it. "Thank you for asking, but right now, I just want to be at home."

Chariss opened her mouth. Chariss closed her mouth. Her shoulders dropped. "Maybe you can come when you're feeling better. I have a ridiculously elegant suite at the Ritz."

"I'll think about it."

"Place Vendôme." She had a carrot on a stick and she was waving it for all she was worth.

"Why?" I asked. "Why now?" Chariss had never demonstrated the slightest inclination to spend time with me.

"You're my daughter."

I shrugged.

"And, we're a disaster."

I didn't disagree.

Chariss looked out the window. She looked at Consuela. She looked at me. "And I love you."

I looked out the window where the waves met the sand. I looked at Consuela who snored softly. I looked at Chariss and looked past the anger and resentment and frustration. "I love you, too."

# TWENTY-SIX

I glanced down at the business card clasped in my fingers then up at the building. Not what I was expecting. Not at all.

I'd conjured up a headquarters to rival James Bond's. The reality was a non-descript beige office building.

I stepped into the empty lobby, pushed the elevator button, and rode to the fifth floor.

The elevator deposited me in a hallway. To my left were the stairs, to my right was a simple door.

I tightened my grip on John Brown's card and pushed the door open.

"May I help you?" A prim receptionist sat at a seen-better-days desk.

I cleared my throat. "I'd like to see Mr. Brown."

She tilted her head like a curious robin. "Mr. Brown?"

"John Brown." I showed her the card. "This is his office, isn't it?"

"Yes, it is." She frowned. "Do you have an appointment?"

"No."

"If you'll have a seat, I'll see if he's available. Your name?"

"Poppy Fields."

Her brows rose and she typed something into the computer on her desk.

I sat and looked at the print hanging on the opposite wall —Monet's *Poppy Field*.

"Excuse me."

I shifted my gaze to the receptionist.

"Mr. Brown is out of the office but he's due back in twenty minutes. Would you mind waiting?"

"That's fine." I'd hand off the flash drive and be done with John Brown and Jake Smith. Forever.

"Would you care for something to drink?"

"Water. Please."

She stood, pushed a button on her computer, disappeared through a door behind her desk, and returned in an instant. "Would you like a glass?"

"The bottle is fine."

She handed me a chilled bottle and resumed her seat.

I read the nameplate on the front of her desk. Ann Jones. Another alias?

"Have you worked here long?"

"Ten years."

Ten years. "You must enjoy your job."

She offered me a tight smile that said she didn't have time for chit-chat.

Okay then. I took out my phone and checked my email. Ruth Gardner had emailed me again. Hardly a surprise. I received an email from her every few hours. She was representing me when it came to requests for interviews and appearances. The current email informed me I'd been invited on the *Tonight Show* and *This Week*.

Ugh. The last thing I wanted was to be on television.

I typed a response. No to the *Tonight Show*. As for *This Week*, I had no objection if she wanted to appear and talk about travel safety concerns.

I peeked at Twitter. I wasn't trending. A relief.

I sipped the water and returned to my inbox. Barclift begged me to consider publishing under my real name. Failing that, did I want to write a memoir about my recent experience? He could sell that manuscript for millions.

No. No memoir.

"Mr. Brown will see you now."

"You said he was out of the office."

"Yes."

"How did he get in?" No one had passed through the reception area.

"I imagine he took the stairs."

The stairs were outside the door.

Either Ann Jones was lying or there was a lot more to John Brown's non-descript office than met the eye.

She rose. "This way, please."

I followed her to an empty conference room and took a seat.

"He'll be with you in just a moment."

"Thank you." I spoke to her retreating back.

The conference room was beige. Beige walls. Beige carpet. A golden-oak stain on a dated conference table. I sipped my water and waited.

"Miss. Fields, to what do we owe the pleasure?" John Brown paused just inside the door, as if he had so little time for me it wasn't worth sitting down.

I reached into my handbag and pulled out the flash drive. "I brought you this."

"What is that?"

I put the little drive down on the table. "Javier Diaz's files on Venti. Everything from the formula to sales projections."

John Brown stood straighter. "How did you get it?"

"It's a long story." It wasn't, but I didn't appreciate his lurking by the doorway.

He took a seat across from me and reached for the drive.

I told him about the second hiding place in Marta's handbag.

"When did you find this?"

"Last night."

He picked up the phone and jabbed out a number. "Ms. Jones, would you please bring us a laptop?"

A moment later, Ms. Jones, prim expression firmly fixed on her face, appeared with a computer.

Mr. Brown logged on and inserted the drive.

His eyes scanned the files and his lips hardened to a firm line. When he finished reading, he shifted his gaze to me. "You've read all of this?"

"I have."

"Then I owe you an apology. Your assessment of Diaz was correct and I dismissed it."

"I get underestimated a lot."

He rubbed his chin. "I bet you do."

I stood. He had the drive and I was done.

"You graduated from USC with honors?"

"Yes."

"Degrees in economics and creative writing?"

"Yes."

"What do you know about money?"

"In the U.S., it's green."

His eyes narrowed. "What do you know about its flow?"

"What do you mean?"

"What do you know about laundering money?"

"Very little. Except—" I stopped myself. The plan was to drop off the drive and leave not converse with John Brown.

"Except what?"

It wasn't like I had any place to be and a small part of me wanted to prove I was more than a pretty face. "Except the resort was owned by a cartel. I assume they overstated everything from occupancy to food and beverage sales."

"A safe assumption."

"And I'm assuming there's a film production company out there that launders money. On a large scale."

"What makes you think that?"

"Call it an educated guess." Brett was working for bad people. I was sure of it. The bank? His clients? Or both? "Of course, to launder really large amounts of money, there needs to be a complicit bank."

John Brown rubbed his chin and stared at me.

"Did I say something wrong?"

"No. Not at all. I'd like to offer you a job."

"A job?"

"You have access to the right people."

"The right people?" Aside from Brett, I was pretty sure I didn't. "What people?"

"People who invest in films and resorts."

"Not really."

"Really. If I sent you to Europe or Asia, you'd be invited to all the right parties. You'd rub shoulders with people we can't hope to approach."

"And then what?"

"You'd tell me what you hear, give me your impressions, ask the right questions."

"It sounds dangerous." I'd had my fill of men like Javier and Ignacio. But more than that, I couldn't stomach the thought of killing someone else.

"It might be."

"Danger is overrated."

Mr. Brown smiled. "True. But you could make a difference. You could help keep drugs out of the hands of children and guns out of the hands of killers."

Make a difference. I could make a difference. I stood. "I'll think about it."

"You have my card."

"I do."

"Next time, call before you come."

I left the office, climbed into my car, and drove away.

It took three blocks (maybe ten) for me to realize I was being followed.

I pressed my foot on the accelerator and flew down the street.

The car behind me did the same.

Damned paparazzi.

The photographer followed me onto the Pacific Coast Highway and drew up next to me.

I looked over, death glare plastered across my face, and saw Jake.

My foot slipped off the accelerator and he shot past me.

Now I followed him, past Malibu and into Oxnard. He pulled into an IHOP parking lot.

IHOP? Pancakes?

The Jake I thought I knew would no more go to an IHOP than he'd wear a plaid sports jacket with a striped tie.

He rolled down his window. "Are you hungry?"

"No."

"How about a cup of coffee? You never say no to coffee." His voice was higher than usual, almost as if he was nervous.

"Fine." I deserved a few answers.

We entered the near empty restaurant, sat in a booth, and stared at each other.

"What can I get you, folks?"

Jake looked up at the waitress. "Coffee. For both of us."

"Say, aren't you that woman who got—"

"Coffee." The expression on Jake's face had her stepping backward.

When she disappeared, I asked, "Why are you following me?"

"You followed me." He handed me a menu. "Are you sure you're not hungry?"

I glanced. Pancakes held zero appeal. "I know what I want."

"What?"

I dropped the menu on the table. "Answers."

The waitress delivered our coffees.

"I'll have a spinach and mushroom omelet," said Jake.

She jotted a note on her pad. "And for you, hon?"

"Just coffee."

She tapped her pad as if she disapproved of customers who didn't eat then walked away.

"You have questions?"

"Yeah."

"Such as?"

"Did you ever care or was it all just part of the job?"

"I can't believe you'd ask me that." His golden aura dulled, hung its head, regarded me with wounded puppy eyes.

I couldn't believe I'd asked that either. The question revealed all sorts of vulnerabilities. A week ago, those words would have been impossible. Now, they just formed a question. I waited.

"Seriously?"

"Seriously. I want an answer."

"I cared." He stared into his coffee as if he'd find words of wisdom floating in the caffeine. "I still care." He shifted his gaze and looked at me with eyes I dared not trust.

I snorted.

"I saved you."

"If you hadn't faked your death, I wouldn't have been in Mexico in the first place."

He had no response for that. Instead, he dug in his pocket. "I have something for you."

Whatever it was, I didn't want it.

He held a fist over the table and waited until I spread my palm. And waited. "Poppy." The way he said my name combined amusement and frustration.

Fine. I'd play along.

Jake dropped my locket into my hand.

"How did you...?"

"Tracking chip. I found it in the mountains."

My throat tightened and my fingers closed around my most precious possession. "Thank you." I glanced up at Jake. "Did you take the chip out?"

"Of course." His response came too quickly.

I didn't believe him. Even with a chip, I fastened the chain around my neck. "You work for Mr. Brown?"

"Yeah. Why?"

"He offered me a job."

*Smack!* The slap of Jake's hand against the table made our coffees jump. The other people in the restaurant (two of whom were wearing pajamas) turned and stared at us.

"Absolutely not! You cannot work for him."

"Why not?"

He leaned forward—almost halfway across the table. "It's too dangerous."

I leaned back—until my back pressed against the booth. "I've proved I'm fairly tough."

"You got lucky."

Maybe I had been lucky. But I'd also turned over those account numbers and the file on Venti. I'd made a difference.

I took a sip of my coffee.

Jake leaned even closer. "You'll get yourself killed." His voice was low and certain.

"Or, you'll get an actual agent killed."

This was the man who'd been the center of my life. And that was what he thought of me. In his eyes, I belonged in a screwball comedy. I wasn't smart enough, or competent enough to be in a thriller. Well, Jake was wrong. I did not belong in some girl-gets-boy comedy. I'd proved that to myself and to Jake's boss. I slid out of the booth.

"Poppy, wait." He caught my wrist and held it.

I cast a frosty gaze at the spot where his skin touched mine.

"I'm sorry. I get a little emotional when I think of you in danger."

"Really?"

There it was, that sun-kissed smile—the one that said I was the center of the universe. "Yeah."

I smiled sweetly and made up my mind. "Get used to being emotional. I'm taking that job."

## ALSO BY JULIE MULHERN

**The Poppy Fields Adventures**

Fields' Guide to Abduction

Fields Guide to Assassins

Fields Guide to Voodoo

**The Country Club Murders**

The Deep End

Guaranteed to Bleed

Clouds in My Coffee

Send in the Clowns

Watching the Detectives

Cold as Ice

Shadow Dancing

Back Stabbers

# ABOUT THE AUTHOR

Julie Mulhern is the USA Today bestselling author of The Country Club Murders and the Poppy Fields Adventures.

She is a Kansas City native who grew up on a steady diet of Agatha Christie. She spends her spare time whipping up gourmet meals for her family, working out at the gym and finding new ways to keep her house spotlessly clean--and she's got an active imagination. Truth is--she's an expert at calling for take-out, she grumbles about walking the dog and the dust bunnies under the bed have grown into dust lions.

Let's stay in touch!